THE GOLDEN

SHOE AWARD

This shoe book
belongs to:

SHOE
WARS

BY Liz Pichon
(Who likes shoes, not WAR.)

SCHOLASTIC PRESS ★ NEW YORK

First published in the United Kingdom in 2020 by Scholastic UK, Euston House,
24 Eversholt Street, London, NW1 1DB, UK, a division of Scholastic Limited.

The publisher does not have any control over and does not assume any responsibility for
author or third-party websites or their content.

Library of Congress Cataloging-in-Publication Data available

ISBN 978-1-338-65474-5

1 2020

Printed in the U.S.A.   23

First US edition, March 2021

For
MARK

(Happy 30th
anniversary!)
♥ ×××

SHOE·PID·I·TY

Wearing shoes that don't fit.

Who knew?

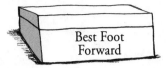

Best Foot
Forward

There's an old saying that goes something like THIS:

You can tell a LOT about a person from the shoes they're wearing...

Random wise person

Do you think that's true?

Take a look at your own

shoes right now.

What do they say about YOU?

Do you like **sports?**

Maybe you enjoy *relaxing*.

Or were you just late for school and got **confused?**

Because some shoes are NOT what they seem to be...

Here are two pairs of shoes.

(Both are important in this story.)

PAIR A have BIG, BULGING EYES,

menacing metal spikes,

a W I D E, gaping

mouth crammed full

of *sharp teeth*, and, if anything gets too close, sensors

that ROAR. These shoes look **scary**. And

if you wore them, you'd definitely stand out in a crowd,

that's for sure.

PAIR B is a nice, neat, flat shoe, the kind you might

wear for school, because teachers LOVE a sensible shoe,

don't they? These are practical

shoes, if boring.

SO, the **IMPORTANT QUESTION** is:

Which pair would YOU choose if you found yourself

in THIS situation? ————————▷

Imagine you're walking down a street, whistling a

happy tune. (If you can't whistle, *SING*.)

SUDDENLY, you hear a dog barking LOUDLY.

You turn around, and it's running toward you,

and NOT in a friendly, pet-my-tummy way.

The closer the dog gets, the angrier it looks—and I mean

FIERCE. Its teeth glisten with dog drool that's

flying out of its MOUTH!

Your first thought is: **GET AWAY!**

As fast as you can before it's too late!

(It is too late, by the way.)

Grrr.

The dog is already at your heels and growling.

You hold your breath and keep completely still, hoping it

doesn't want to bite you.

(It does want to bite you.)

The dog narrows its eyes and begins to move closer.

It's getting ready to JUMP UP

and sink its TEETH right into

your BIG . . .

JUICY . . .

rrrr

. . . WAIT!

Let's STOP everything right there for a second.

HUH?

If you had to pick one pair of shoes to PROTECT

your feet from the VICIOUS DOG, which shoes

would YOU choose?

PAIR A:
the SCARY-LOOKING
SHOES

or PAIR B:
the SENSIBLE-LOOKING
SHOES

In case you need it, here's some more thinking time:

PING! Time's up.

Did you pick PAIR A, the **SCARY-LOOKING**

SHOES, the ones with the metal spikes, SHARP teeth,

and the sensors?

Then you'd be COMPLETELY and utterly . . .

. . . **wrong!** And here's why.

First, they belong to someone named

Wendy Wedge, and if you stole her

shoes, she'd be FURIOUS!

Wendy would send out one of her MEAN,

crazy dogs to get them back.

Second,

JUST LOOK AT THEM!

They're spiky, clumpy, weird, and wobbly.

WHO could even walk, let alone *RUN*, in a pair of

shoes like that?

(Apart from Wendy Wedge, of course.)

BUT if you picked **PAIR B?**

Well, these shoes might not

look like anything special, but they really are.

All you'd have to do to ESCAPE Wendy's dog is

click your heels together and say,

"SHOES UP!"

Then *WHOOOOSSSSHHHH!*

Off you'd go like a ROCKET, and the dog would

be left wondering where you were and biting on

SNAP

nothing but air, because these shoes can FLY!

(HOW exciting is that?)

Imagine the FUN you could have wearing flying shoes.

Ding Ding Ding

You'd never be late for school again.

Reaching anything high would be EASY!

Looking over tall people's heads?

No problem at all!

Flying shoes would be **AMAZING.**

EVERYONE would want a pair (including me).

But . . . (There's always a "but," isn't there?)

Before you get too excited about the shoes, the person who owns them doesn't want ANYONE to know they even EXIST.

ESPECIALLY not one person in particular:

Wendy Wedge.

(Yes, HER again.)

Because if SHE found out about the shoes, it would be a

DISASTER!

First, Wendy would STEAL the shoes. Then she would LIE and say that SHE invented them. Then, being a **REAL** meany, she'd USE them to ENTER the MOST prestigious competition EVER—

THE GOLDEN SHOE AWARDS.

(Wendy Wedge is so desperate to win, it hurts.)

Every FOUR years, the VERY BEST shoemaking towns are INVITED to compete for the **ultimate** SHOE prize.

At the BIG, *GLITZY* ceremony, the competition is always FIERCE. The most inventive and incredible shoes with gadgets are presented to the panel of judges.

THE GOLDEN SHOE AWARDS

A winning pair of shoes can change the luck AND lives of the inventors **FOREVER**.

So far, this has NOT happened to Wendy Wedge.

She enters every single competition. But she's only won a prize once, for **BEST JOKE SHOE** . . .

and even that was a mistake.

It's not like Wendy hasn't tried to win

THE GOLDEN SHOE AWARD.

Her kind of clunky, thick WEDGES just hasn't

impressed the judges.

But with a pair of FLYING SHOES, first

PRIZE would be HERS, and no one could

laugh at her ever again.

Wendy would become even MORE

powerful and VILE than she is now,

and WHO KNOWS what other dastardly deeds she'd

get up to?

So you understand why keeping these shoes hidden is

REALLY important. And so far they've

been a VERY well-kept secret.

Right up until now . . .

. . . when EVERYTHING is about to change.

(The dog's still fine, in case you were worried.

Look at its happy little face.)

Size One

SHOE TOWN was famous for one thing

. . . melons. (I'm kidding—it's shoes, of course.)

Ivor Foot lived there with his two children, **Ruby** and

Bear, in the **Shoebox neighborhood** in a small house that

was shaped like—you guessed it—a shoebox.

One night, when most people in the neighborhood

were fast asleep, a slightly odd sound began to $WAFT$

out of the Foot family's house.

It was a sort of . . . **WHOOSH**

whooosh **WHOOSHING noise** . . .

It woke Ruby up.

She was used to hearing noises what with all the

shoebox houses being so close together, but for some

reason, this felt different and she wasn't sure why.

Ruby kept listening.

WHOOooooSHhhhh
WHOOOooooSH
WHOOSHHHHH

There it was again.

 "Bear . . . BEAR!" Ruby called

out to her brother, who was asleep on

the other side of the room they shared. He didn't answer,

so Ruby got up. Bear could sleep through anything,

which Ruby found annoying.

"BEAR, did you hear that?" Ruby gave him a

good shake.

"I'm asleep," he grumbled.

"No, you're not," Ruby pointed out.

"I am," Bear mumbled, and turned over.

"Bear . . ." Ruby kept SHAKING him.

"Go back to bed," Bear told her.

Then she heard the NOISE again.

WHOOOooooSHhhhh
WHOOOoooSH
WHOOSHHHHH

"**What is it?**" Ruby asked, leaning over him.

"**Probably a . . . monster,**" Bear told her sleepily.

"**Funny. I'm going to get Dad up,**" Ruby said.

"**Don't wake up Dad.**" Bear sighed, but Ruby ignored

him (she did that a lot).

She slid open their bedroom door and saw light

coming from the kitchen.

Good, Dad's already awake, Ruby thought. But it

sounded like someone else was with him. She could hear

talking.

Who was it?

Ruby crept down the hallway and stepped over the creaky bits on the floor. Then she hid behind the bookcase (her secret place to listen to grown-up chats without being seen).

Pushing a thick cookbook to one side left a nice gap for her to peer into the kitchen. Ruby couldn't see Dad—but she could hear him talking.

"NO one can EVER find out about these shoes. NOT Ruby, NOT Bear, and most importantly, NOT WENDY WEDGE!

If SHE EVER got her hideous hands or horrible feet on these shoes it would be a *DISASTER!*"

Ruby froze. Dad sounded serious.

Wendy Wedge was Dad's terrible boss and Ruby didn't like her at all (not many people did).

What shoes? I can keep a secret! Ruby thought.

She was even MORE curious now.

Ruby listened carefully as dad kept talking.

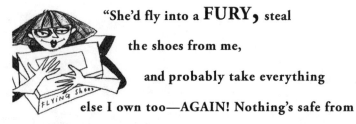 "She'd fly into a **FURY,** steal

the shoes from me,

and probably take everything

else I own too—AGAIN! Nothing's safe from

WENDY WEDGE! Not even YOU, Shoo."

So *that's* who Dad was talking to!

Shoo was their cat, who often got stuck on top of

the cupboard. Maybe Dad was rescuing her?

Ruby leaned forward as far as she could.

"You know what, Shoo? With a little more work,

I think we COULD WIN the Golden Shoe Award.

Imagine the look on Wendy's face,"

 Dad said—then his voice got sadder.

"It was always Sally's DREAM to win

the award—she invented these shoes

when we owned the shop. Sally worked

on the plans for years until they were almost perfect."

Dad sighed loudly.

"If it hadn't been for that snake, things would be so different. I wouldn't be working for Wendy Wedge, THAT'S for sure."

Shoo *m e o w e d* like she was answering

Dad back.

Ruby kept quiet. Dad was talking about Mom.

She missed her mom too. Ruby and Bear were only little when their mom died from a rare, poisonous snakebite.

It was a mystery where the snake had come from, and no one knew where it had gone.

"Come on, Shoo, that's enough excitement for one night. Let's get you down," Dad said.

Ruby blinked a few times—and watched as SOMETHING floated down from the ceiling. Was she seeing things?

"Whoooaahh . . ."

Ruby's mouth dropped open.

Size Two

Ruby stared as

TWO FEET

hovered in the air.

Then, slowly,

they dropped

down,

lower

and

lower

and

lower.

IT WAS DAD!

BUT IT was the **SHOES** he was wearing that REALLY

got her attention.

On each side of each shoe was a small

white feather wing that was fluttering up and down

and making THAT

whoooosshing whoooossh

whooshing noise.

Ruby stared as Dad brought the shoes down to land.

She wanted to SHOUT,

"This IS SO **EXCITING!**

DAD'S GOT FLYING SHOES!"

She'd NEVER seen flying shoes before. No one had.

They were supposed to be *impossible* to make!

As Dad got closer to the ground, he

SUDDENLY began to

LURCH *one way*

and then the other.

Then his feet behind to **wobble,**

and

SWAY . . .

. . . from side

. . . to side.

"Ooooppppps!

Come on, shoes . . .

not now . . .

Shoes DOWN.

Shoes DOWN.

Nicely does it."

Finally, Dad got things under control and landed safely.

"Rescue complete," he declared as Shoo leaped from his arms onto the floor. Ruby rubbed her eyes.

WAS this REALLY HAPPENING? She had a million questions to ask Dad now, like:

Did you MAKE the flying shoes?

How high can they fly?

Can I get my OWN pair?

How FAST can they go?

And MOST importantly—

WHY DIDN'T YOU TELL US ABOUT

THE FLYING SHOES BEFORE!

Ruby was about to slide back out from behind

the bookshelves to get answers

when **something** Dad said instantly STOPPED her.

"Ruby and Bear MUST **NEVER EVER** know about these flying shoes. One day I'll be able to tell them the whole story of how they were made—but it's too risky now."

Dad picked up a photo of Mom.

"You'd be really proud of them, Sally. They're fantastic kids—a bit pesky, but they get that from you—obviously." Dad laughed.

There were lots of photos of Mom around the house. The one Dad was holding was Ruby's favorite. Sally's death had made the news, as snakes had never been seen before in Shoe Town.

Sally Sandal at work.

Ruby's mom and dad had run a shoe shop together that sold Sally's amazing inventions. They all lived above the shop. But after Sally died, Dad got sad and stopped making any shoes or running the shop. His good friends Betty Boot and Bert Brogue had

I brought a casserole

tried their very best to help out, but nothing could STOP Wendy Wedge from *SWOOPING* in like a VULTURE to make Dad an offer that was hard to refuse.

"Sell me your shop and everything in it, and I'll give you a job at World of Wedge, and a house in the Shoebox neighborhood too, because I am a very good person* and I CARE DEEPLY about you and your family," she'd told him. **"Think of your CHILDREN, Ivor. Sign here and ALL your problems will DISAPPEAR."**

Wendy had lied.

*Foot note: Wendy was not a very good person.

The contract was SUPER LONG with a LOT of conditions written in teeny-tiny writing.

Dad was in a terrible position.

He really needed the money and didn't feel like he had a choice.

"We need time to pack. I'm keeping everything Sally made," Dad had insisted. Then, with Wendy's grizzly dogs growling at his feet, Dad had reluctantly signed.

SIGN HERE
Ivor Foot

The family had barely moved out

when Wendy arranged for the whole shoe shop

... to be knocked down.

Luckily, Ivor had managed to rescue the FLYING

SHOES and keep them away from Wendy. Those shoes

had become even MORE precious to Ivor now that he

no longer had his wonderful Sally, his sole mate, by his

side. He was determined to keep them safe, along with

her books and a few other possessions.

Now, Ivor glanced at the clock. It was after 2:30 a.m.

He began putting the shoes away in their wooden box.

 Bedtime... **"Come on, Shoo, we both need to get some rest,"** he said. **"That's enough excitement for one night. Let's go check on the kids and make sure they're still asleep."**

Ruby gulped. "Uh-oh . . ."

She had to go **NOW** before Dad saw,

and there wasn't much time.

Ruby slid out from behind the

bookcase and quickly tiptoed down the hall, avoiding

the creaky floorboards back to her room, where Bear

was still asleep and snoring quietly.

Ruby **jumped** under the covers

and pulled them over her head. She was followed

closely by Shoo, who then decided it was a good idea to

L E A P onto Ruby's bed and

start pressing her paws UP and DOWN

like she was kneading dough.

"Get off me, Shoo!" Ruby hissed,

but Shoo wouldn't budge.

SHOO!

Ruby pretended to be asleep when Dad came in. He checked Bear was okay, then walked over to Ruby and gently lifted Shoo up. Ruby stayed very still and didn't move.

"Night-night, Ruby and Bear. Sleep tight, don't wear your shoes too tight," Dad whispered, then carried Shoo out and slid the door shut.

Ruby waited for a few seconds before she breathed OUT and her EYES pinged WIDE open. HOW could she go to sleep NOW?

All she could think about was . . .

FLYING SHOES.

Flying shoes with white feather wings!

Flying shoes flying up and down.

Dad had flying shoes!

Should she tell Bear? Or would he BLAB?

It was supposed to be a secret after all.

Her mind was BUZZING, but it was so late that her eyes slowly began to get heavier . . . and heavier . . . and heavier.

Until . . .

flying . . . shoes . . .

shoes . . . flying shoes . . .

chocolate . . . choco . . . late . . .

Mmmmmmmmm.

Flying chocolate

Size Three

"Wakey, Wakey!"

Bear leaned over Ruby and gave her a little shake.

He was already dressed and ready for school.

"I'm awake," she told him, groaning.

"It's annoying when someone wakes you up,

isn't it?" Bear smirked.

Ruby bolted upright as she remembered—

the FLYING SHOES!

"You look like a zombie. That's what happens when

you get up in the middle of the night," Bear said, and

POKED her, which was ANNOYING.

Without thinking, Ruby replied, **"WELL, YOU**

missed out by NOT getting up, because I saw . . ."

"What?" asked Bear.

"Err, nothing," said Ruby.

Bear made a face at her.

"You saw . . . A **MONSTER!**"

he roared, trying to scare her.

"**Funny,**" Ruby said, glaring at him and

NOT laughing.

"**Okay. I'll just ask Dad.**"

"**No, don't!**" she shouted.

Bear looked at her carefully.

"**What are you hiding, Ruby?**"

"**Nothing, I just need to get ready for school.**

And if you don't stop BUGGING me,

I'll sing your favorite song."

"**DON'T SING!**"

Bear covered his ears.

Singing was Ruby's secret weapon to annoy him.

"Too late!" she shouted, and BURST

into song. **"Chips! What do we want?**

We want CHIPS!

When do we want them? Now!"

Bear put his hands over his ears.

"That stupid SONG will be STUCK in my

head all day now," he said, and stomped out

of the room.

Ruby stopped singing and sighed. She knew there was

no way Bear would let this go. He never forgot anything.

Bear had an amazing memory for all kinds of weird facts,

odd things, and peculiar creatures.

She pulled the lever to open up her wardrobe, and

the clothing rack shot out. It was messy, but Ruby knew

where everything was.

Their whole house was filled with all kinds of unusual space-saving gadgets and quirky pieces of furniture: chairs that turned into tables, tables that pulled out from walls, and shelves that spun around to become pictures.

SWOOSH

Over the years, their dad had made ordinary objects EXTRAORDINARY, and nothing was what it seemed to be. It was a small house, but what it lacked in space, it made up for in style, **imagination**, and color, everywhere.

Ruby got dressed and pulled the lever again.

Her clothing rack glided back into the box with a nice

satisfying S w o o o s h h h h i n g sound.

She grabbed her schoolbag and pretended

to skate her way to the kitchen in her socks.

Bear and Dad were having breakfast at the table. The

top was covered in Mom's hand-painted tiles, and each tile

showed a different shoe from their old shop on it—the kind

of shoes not easy to find in **SHOE TOWN** anymore.

There were comfy cloud shoes, shoes that looked

like sandwiches with a secret

compartment to keep snacks in,

super-SPEEDY shoes with wheels and lights,

useful shoes with storage

drawers in the heels,

and pencil shoes with some handy notepaper attached.

There were even fish-shaped shoes.

No wedges, though.

Ruby noticed that Dad looked more tired than usual.

(She knew why.)

"Morning, Ruby. Did you sleep okay?" he asked her.

Before she could answer, Bear interrupted.

"Nope. Ruby woke ME up and then she wanted to wake YOU up too, Dad."

"No, I didn't!" Ruby protested.

"Were you awake last night?" Dad asked her.

"I thought I heard a noise, but it was just Bear snoring." Ruby shrugged like it was nothing.

ZZZZZZ

"I don't snore . . ." Bear told her.

"You do TOO—like a WARTHOG."

Ruby snorted to show him what he sounded like.

"Ha! That sounds more like ME!" Dad laughed,

then cleared his throat. **"Hey, listen, you two. I've got a**

surprise for you. BUT you have to PROMISE me

that you won't tell anyone. It has to be our secret."

Ruby sat up and paid attention. Was Dad going to

tell them about the flying shoes?

"What is it, Dad?" Bear asked.

"Well, it's about the NEW school shoes you all

have to wear now."

Ruby and Bear groaned.

"Wendy calls them her WOWs—that's World

of Wedge shoes."

"Ugh. World of STUPID SHOES, more like. Why can't we wear USEFUL shoes to school, like THESE?" Bear pointed to the table tile of the shoe with speedy wheels and lights.

"Or cloud shoes. They'd be all FLUFFY and SO comfy!" Ruby agreed.

"I know these WOWs aren't very comfortable—"

"You can say that again," Bear interrupted, grumbling. "WOWs should stand for Worst Ordinary Wobbly shoes—ever. AND they're really hard to run around in too," he added.

"I'm sorry, guys, it's the school rules," Dad continued. "But I knew you wouldn't be happy about wearing them, so I've made a few ADJUSTMENTS, even though I'm not supposed to."

Ruby and Bear stopped eating and looked at each other in excitement.

"Wait here, I'll be right back," Dad said.

As soon as he left, Ruby turned to Bear and whispered, **"I know what Dad's done to our school shoes."**

"What?" he asked.

"Last night, when I woke up, **I saw something AMAZING."**

"You did?"

"YES! Dad was in the kitchen, and you'll NEVER guess what he was wearing . . ." She paused to make her brother wait a little longer.

"Tell me!" Bear demanded.

"GUESS!"

"Ruby!" Bear sighed.

"Flying shoes! Isn't that FANTASTIC?!"

Bear stared at her suspiciously.

"Are you sure?" he asked.

"YES! IT'S TRUE! Dad was flying around the kitchen UP in the AIR."

Ruby clapped her hands together and made Shoo jump.

"Ruby—everyone knows flying shoes don't ACTUALLY exist. Even Dad said that. It's a FACT. LOTS of people have tried to create them over the years, but everyone's failed," Bear told her. "The last town who tried to enter **THE GOLDEN SHOE AWARDS** with flying shoes was Shoe Jersey. Their synchronized flying team didn't even get off the ground."

Not flying

Ruby shrugged. "Well, Mom managed to do it, and Dad has been keeping them a secret from Wendy Wedge all this time."

"I guess that makes sense. She IS really mean." Bear tipped his head thoughtfully.

"SO, when Dad comes back we HAVE to act surprised, like we had **NO** idea he's turned our boring old school shoes into flying shoes, okay?"

Bear nodded. **"Okay—how's this, then?"**

He made a SURPRISED face.

"Not bad," said Ruby.

"Maybe a little over the top."

"Or this?" Bear tried again.

"Better." She grinned, just as

Dad came back holding their

NEW, IMPROVED school shoes. Which looked

exactly the same as the old ones.

Ruby and Bear put on their innocent "we know

nothing" faces.

"What have you done, Dad?" Bear asked.

"Just a few little CHANGES. You don't want to

attract any attention, remember?" Dad said.

46

"I'm good at keeping secrets!" Ruby smiled.

Bear gave her a look, unconvinced.

"WHAT? I am!" she muttered.

"Now here's what you need to do," said Dad.

Ruby turned to Bear and mouthed the word "FLY" at

him.

"There's a secret pad inside each shoe,

and if you SCRUNCH UP all your toes

together . . ." Dad began to explain.

"Yes?" they chorused excitedly.

"At exactly the same time . . ."

"Yes?" they said again.

"You'll be able to . . ."

(. . . *FLY!* Ruby was thinking.)

"... trigger the EXTRA-SQUISHY inner soles that will mold to your feet and make your shoes SO comfy. Its special fluffiness makes you feel like you're walking on AIR," Dad told them both.

"Oh." Ruby couldn't hide her disappointment. "Um. Is there anything else they can do, Dad?" she asked hopefully.

"Just a few more things. THIS part's really good, if I do say so myself. You need to lean back

on your heels. Right one first, then the left. That activates a HEATING pad for the cold winter days," Dad told them, hoping they'd be excited.

"Um," said Ruby. "Anything else?"

"Oh YES! How could I forget. You can also . . ."

(FLY! FLY! FLY!)

48

"BOUNCE really high. I've put special springs inside to make every step you take extra bouncy. It's good for running. Just don't overdo it," Dad told them.

Ruby and Bear stared at each other and then at the shoes.

"Is that all?" Ruby said.

"Don't you like the changes?" Dad looked at them, confused.

"We do!" Bear said. **"It's just that I got really excited because Ruby told me you'd added—"**

"WHEELS!" Ruby shouted,

cutting Bear off.

"NO, not WHEELS. You said—"

"LIGHTS! I REALLY WANTED SHOES THAT

LIGHT UP—SO BADLY!" Ruby yelled,

and GLARED at Bear to

make him STOP talking.

"I guess I can add those later,"

Dad said, slightly confused at their LACK of enthusiasm.

 "Thanks, Dad, they're great,"

Ruby told him.

"Right," Dad said, standing up. "You two

go and brush your teeth. I'll get my work things."

As soon as they were out of earshot, Bear turned to

Ruby. "WHAT was that about? WHY did you keep

talking over me?"

"Because I was wrong. Dad didn't make

flying shoes for US."

"Obviously," Bear said with a sigh.

"PLEASE don't tell him I saw him flying? Not yet,"

Ruby begged.

"And did you? Really?" Bear asked.

"YES!" Ruby snapped. "If you

don't believe me, I'll prove it.

The shoes must be HERE in the house somewhere."

"Why can't we just ask Dad about them?" Bear suggested.

"Because I HEARD him say 'Ruby and Bear

must NEVER find out about the flying shoes.'

So please don't say anything, okay?"

"All right, I won't." Bear lowered his

voice. "Besides, I might even know where Dad keeps

them. He has a secret workshop."

"Where? Come on, tell me.

I can keep a secret!" Ruby pleaded.

"You really can't."

"Pinkie promise . . ." said Ruby, holding out her little

finger to Bear.

"ALL RIGHT. I'll show you after school," he agreed.

They linked their little fingers together and made a pinkie promise just as Dad came back and saw them.

"What are you two up to?"

"Just making sure we don't say ANYTHING about our new shoes," Ruby said quickly.

"Good thinking. I like a pinkie promise. After all, we don't need any trouble* at school, do we?" Dad said cheerfully.

"As if we'd get into any trouble, Dad," Bear said, looking him RIGHT in the eye.

"That would NEVER happen, Dad," Ruby added enthusiastically.

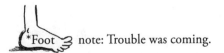 *Foot note: Trouble was coming.

52

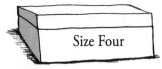

Size Four

Dad, Ruby, and Bear left the house together.

Ruby and Bear were finding their new school shoes more fun than they'd expected. They might not fly, but, BOY, could they **bounce.**

"Dad, these shoes are SO GOOD!" Ruby told him as she bounced up and down.

"Easy, you two, we don't want them getting too much attention," Dad said, trying to get them to calm down. He could already see that Mrs. Court from across the road was heading their way. She'd recently moved to the neighborhood, so no one knew much about her. But every time anyone left the house, Mrs. Court would APPEAR in an instant—like she'd been waiting for them.

Mrs. Court wore bright **red** cat-eye glasses that matched her bright **red** lipstick, and her dark hair was piled up in a BUN on top of her head.

She used a walking stick to help her get around and for other things too, like pushing open her gate,

shooing away birds, and knocking on people's doors. Right now, Mrs. Court was standing in front of them tapping her heels on the ground.

She didn't look happy.

"**Good morning, Mrs. Court. Have you settled in?**" Ivor asked politely.

"**Mr. Foot, there were some strange NOISES coming from your house last night. It was very, very late,**" Mrs. Court told him, frowning.

"**Are you SURE it was our house? We were all fast asleep, weren't we, kids?**" Ivor said quickly.

He took a step forward, but Mrs. Court stuck out her walking stick to block their way.

"**Mr. Foot, SOMETHING was going on. I didn't move here to be disturbed by noisy neighbors.**"

"**I completely understand,**" Dad said soothingly. "**Well, I have to get to work. And these two need to be at school. It's a busy day today.**" He smiled, then tried to edge past.

But Mrs. Court hadn't finished.

She pressed a button on the top

of her walking stick, and a sharp point

appeared from the end.

"Whoaa . . ." Ruby was impressed.

Mrs. Court then proceeded to SPEAR some dead

leaves from the ground with a quick

jabbing movement.

Once she'd collected them, she

pressed the button again and PINGED

the leaves OFF into a nearby trash can.

"I don't like messes," Mrs. Court told them.

"MESSINESS was never a problem

back in Shoehampton."

"Messiness can be a problem in our house!" Ivor joked.

Mrs. Court looked at Ivor suspiciously. **"I didn't realize you were from Shoehampton, Mrs. Court. The winners of THE GOLDEN SHOE AWARD for the last three years. You could give Wendy Wedge a few tips on how to win."** Ivor laughed.

"I've heard she can be a very *difficult* person," Mrs. Court replied slowly, peering over her glasses.

"You could say that," Dad agreed.

"She just did, Dad," Ruby pointed out.

"Which is why we must go! I don't want to be late for work," Ivor said, and turned to leave.

Mrs. Court lifted her walking stick up and tapped it three times on the ground. The stick shrank into her hand until it was half its size, then she popped it into her handbag.

Mrs. Court strolled back into her house, and called over her shoulder, **"No more noise, please, Mr. Foot. I like peace and quiet, remember."**

Dad waved. **"Lovely to talk to you, Mrs. Court,"** he muttered.

"It wasn't that lovely," Bear mumbled.

"She's tricky," Ruby whispered. **"Her walking stick was awesome, though. I'd like one of those,"** she told Bear as they watched Mrs. Court close her door.

"Come on, kids, let's go. I need to impress Wendy with the wedges I've been working on for THE GOLDEN SHOE AWARDS. Today is the big presentation and we're all under pressure, so I can't be late."

"The camera wedges you made are THE BEST, Dad! I loved playing with them," Ruby told him.

"You PLAYED with them?" Dad sounded surprised.

"A little bit . . ." Ruby said. **"Bear and I both did. They were fun! Dad, if Wendy doesn't like those wedges, she's a fool!"** That made Dad laugh.

"They were really excellent, Dad. Wendy would be STUPID not to pick yours," Bear added.

"Well, I just hope Wendy likes them as much as you guys do. She's hard to please."

"I don't like Wendy Wedge." Ruby scowled.

"Shhhhhhh! Keep your voice down, you never know who's listening," Dad whispered. He looked up at the HUGE W-shaped building that cast an eerie shadow over their entire neighborhood.

"Come on, let's go," Ivor said with a shiver.

As they walked quickly past one of the many HUGE posters around **SHOE TOWN** for **THE GOLDEN SHOE AWARDS**, Dad stopped to remind Ruby and Bear one more time.

"So remember—not a word about your special gadget school shoes. As far as you're concerned, they're just PLAIN, ordinary shoes and there's nothing unusual about them at all."

Ivor hugged them both and watched as they bounced into school.

I'm higher than you.

LOOK! I'm BOUNCING.

"YOU TWO! STOP BOUNCING!" Ivor called out, then turned toward the BIG gates of the WOW building. Ivor knew it was going to be a difficult day, and he gave himself a minute to imagine how furious Wendy would be if she knew about Sally's flying shoes, and that cheered him up.

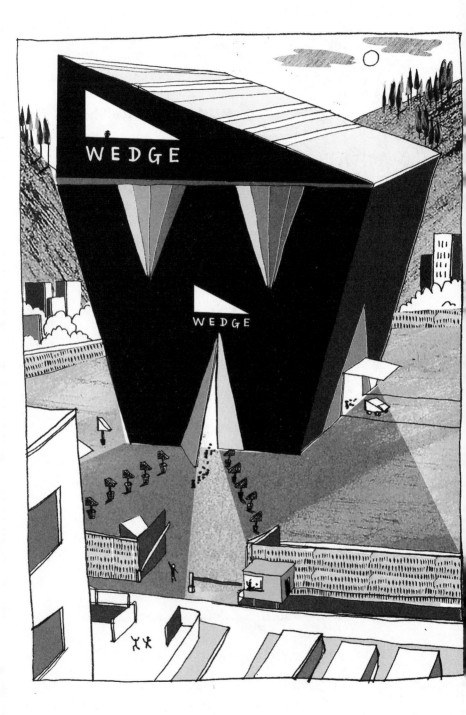

Size Five

At exactly the same time as Ivor was going into WOW,

Walter Wedge (Wendy's terrible son) was walking out.

He was NOT smiling (nothing NEW there).

Walter stomped toward the school accompanied by

Wendy's assistant, Mr. Creeper, who didn't look happy

either. Ruby and Bear were forced to stand back as Walter

pushed past.

Walter Wedge was Wendy's only son and not very nice

at all. (That's putting it lightly.)

Walter's idea of having fun was to RUIN everyone

else's. And if you think I'm exaggerating, this is what he's

been up to in just the last few days:

(There's not enough time to tell you EVERYTHING, but you'll

get the idea.)

Pushed a boy's ice cream into his face;

helped himself to another kid's

toys, then broke them on purpose;

CRUSHED UP chips in their bags,

just for FUN;

kicked a soccer ball over a high wall to wreck a game;

ruined a kid's birthday party (that he WASN'T invited to)

by popping the balloons,

pouring water over the cake,

helping himself to the food,

and, worst of all . . .

OPENING the presents!

Does Walter EVER get told off?

NO. Or hardly ever. Once, his mother got angry when

he ruined a pair of

her favorite wedges, but

that was a long time ago.

Walter discovered that the worse he behaved, the more attention his mother gave him. So he just kept on doing it. NO ONE was allowed to say a BAD word about Walter, especially not in front of Wendy. She was such an important and powerful person in **Shoe Town** that people were careful not to upset her. Everyone just put up with Walter's rotten behavior.

Wendy and Walter were known around town as the **Gruesome** Twosome. (Not to their faces—OBVIOUSLY.) When Walter was little, Wendy decided he was too advanced to mix with any other children, so she hired tutors to teach him at home. But thanks to Walter's AWFUL attitude, none of the tutors EVER stayed for long. I mean, why would they? What right-minded teacher would put up with being SOAKED by a bucket of water sneakily placed on top of the door? Or being given a delicious, red, rosy apple by Walter . . .

. . . only to find HALF a **FAT**, JUICY worm inside.

(You can guess where the other HALF was.)

How Walter would **laugh!**

And when his tutors finally left (as they always did), Walter would let the dogs out to say goodbye.

Playing pranks made Walter happy—but that cheerful feeling never seemed to last very long.

Bored by playing with fancy games and gadgets on his own, Walter would sit in his HUGE bedroom gazing out his window at the children of **Shoe Town** as they laughed and skipped into school.

"WHY are they having MORE fun than me? And what's so good about stupid SHOE SCHOOL anyway? It's not FAIR—I WANT TO GO THERE TOO!"

Walter had DEMANDED.

Reluctantly, Wendy had agreed, mostly because finding

any new tutors had become an impossible task. (If you're

starting to feel sorry for Walter, don't. He gets worse.)

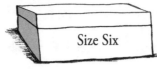

Size Six

Wendy ordered the Shoe School principal,

Mr. Moccasin, to come to WOW footquarters.

She sat Mr. Moccasin in the smallest, squeakiest,

and MOST uncomfortable chair. (Wendy

enjoyed making people feel awkward.) As Walter would be

mixing with "ordinary" children, she insisted that her

little darling be looked after.

Wendy told Mr. Moccasin how smart Walter was and

how LUCKY the school would be to have him. And that

wasn't all.

"Walter needs a special desk," Wendy explained.

"Adjusted to the exact right height and a chair to

match. He has wonderful posture, like me, and I want

to keep it that way. No one

likes a sloucher.

"Walter ALSO needs his own personal play space and should be excused from anything he doesn't want to do. And for goodness' sake, put him in a class with children who have a brain. I don't want his finely tuned mind turning to MUSH."

Mr. Moccasin listened carefully and then replied, **"Ms. Wedge, of course we'll look after Walter and I'm sure he'll thoroughly enjoy being part of our wonderful school. But I can't promise everything you're asking. We do have OTHER children to think about."**

(Which was brave of him.)

"Oh, REALLY?" Wendy said, and raised an EYEBROW. She was not very impressed.

GENIUS

"Maybe THIS might help you FOCUS on MY son a little more?" Wendy THUMPED a briefcase stuffed full of money onto the table. She pushed it over to Mr. Moccasin and GLARED at him.

"I'm SURE your wonderful school could do with a few improvements here and there. New equipment? More books? A new desk for YOU, perhaps?"

Mr. Moccasin looked at the CASH and swallowed. "Well . . . I don't know what to say, that's very generous of you . . ." he managed to answer.

Wendy nodded. "Isn't it? We can discuss renaming the school in my honor later."

"Oh, I'm not sure about THAT . . ." Mr. Moccasin began. Wendy swiftly reached over and PULLED the money back toward her.

"Think of the school trips, the heated swimming pool. THINK of the CHILDREN, Mr. Moccasin."

Wendy made a sad face.

Mr. Moccasin was feeling the pressure. Wendy was making it clear he didn't really have a choice. WOW was a very powerful company in **SHOE TOWN** and growing larger by the day.

"Yes, that's a wonderful idea, Ms. Wedge," Mr. Moccasin quickly corrected himself.

Wendy pushed the money back toward him and smiled. **"And one more thing,"** she said. **"The constant noise of the children running around? I can't BEAR it. I can HEAR everything from WOW footquarters."**

"But it's impossible to stop the children from moving or talking, Ms. Wedge," Mr. Moccasin explained.

"NOTHING'S impossible," snapped Wendy. **"And I have the PERFECT solution."**

"**You do?**" Mr. Moccasin asked nervously.

"**Yes. ALL the children will wear brand-new shoes of my own design,**" Wendy told Mr. Moccasin. Her hand hovered over the CASH.

CLUMPY
shoes

"**They're nice and quiet and only *slightly* uncomfortable. So no more noise, a lot less running, and hopefully we can CUT down on all that annoying laughter and FUN.**"

Mr. Moccasin was speechless.

"**Oh, and Walter will wear his OWN special WOWs.**"

(Of course he will.)

Mr. Moccasin pulled himself together and thought about EVERYTHING she'd said. It wasn't EASY, but he told Wendy that Walter would be welcomed into the school just like any other child in **SHOE TOWN**.

"He's NOT like any other child, though—

Walter is a GENIUS. He's a mini ME," Wendy corrected him. **"And you**

would do well to remember that."

Mr. Moccasin took a deep

breath and told himself that Walter was only a small boy.

After all, how bad could he be?*

*Foot note: VERY BAD.

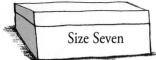

Size Seven

Walter had arrived for his FIRST

day of school clutching two

bags STUFFED full of . . .

PRANKS.

He'd gotten to work right away—

not with books or pens, but by

making TROUBLE.

Walter thought HE was HILARIOUS.

(No one else did.)

Putting up with Walter just became part of the

school day, because EVERYONE knew

> I know
> it's fake,
> Walter . . .

who his mother was. And after a

few weeks of playing the SAME

pranks on the SAME kids, Walter got bored. He'd

stomped around and insisted on being moved to a different

class. And, of course, Walter always got what he wanted.

(No one was sorry to see him go.)

So today Walter was excited to have a FRESH bunch of kids to torment. He was looking forward to having some fun. As soon as Bear saw the fancy new chair and plush cushion next to his desk, he knew something was up. **"Oh no,"** he sighed when he read the name on the cushion.

But the sight of Walter striding toward him with his sharp black bangs and menacing stare, looking like a small version of Wendy (in pants), was still alarming. Walter BOWED like he was royalty, then said, **"I'm here now—get used to it,"** before sitting down.

The school day began peacefully enough. Their teacher, Miss Mule, had assigned them a writing project, and they were all working away quietly, when Bear got up to get more paper. Walter took the opportunity to play his favorite prank. He was laughing before Bear even sat down. Paaaarrrrrrrppppppp!

Ha! Ha! Ha!

"What's funny?" Bear asked him.

"Oh . . ." Bear rolled his eyes, then handed the whoopee cushion back to Walter. "I think this belongs to you." Bear smiled weakly.

"Funny, right? And I'm just getting started," Walter bragged.

"I can tell," Bear said, and Walter laughed some more.

"Watch this—it always works," he said, and took out a FAKE spider (one of many he owned).

He THREW the spider into the middle of

the room, where it landed on Freddie Flat's face.

"AGHHHHHHHHHH!"

Freddie screamed.

"What's going on?" Miss Mule demanded.

Walter kept quiet and smirked.

Bear had the feeling that today wasn't going to be easy.*

*Foot note: THAT was putting it mildly.

Back at the **SHOEBOX** HOUSE . . .

MUCH later on . . .

things had been happening.

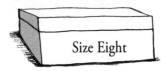

Size Eight

Ivor Foot was in trouble.

THIS is how much trouble

Ivor was in . . .

An

ENTIRE

two-

page

spread's

worth

of

trouble . . .

(Which is a lot.)

He'd come home to find a
few white feathers on the floor
of Ruby and Bear's bedroom.

*Maybe they had a pillow
fight?* Ivor thought.

Or perhaps he had dropped them himself? It was
probably nothing. But Ivor decided to make sure the
flying shoes were safe—just in case.

He went into the kitchen and peeked out the

window to check that nobody was
around, especially nosy Mrs. Court,
then went to the table covered in
pictures of shoes. Ivor picked up a

vase of slightly wilting flowers and put it on the floor—
gently. The kids had picked the flowers last week as a
present for him.

Surprise!

"Right," he muttered, studying the table. **"Come on, Ivor—remember the combination."**

The mosaic tabletop had been designed by Sally. And it HID something SPECTACULAR.

Pressing the shoe tiles down in the RIGHT order would open up Ivor's secret workroom. He could NEVER remember what the right order was, though.

Ivor was so busy trying to get the combination right that he didn't notice that the water in the vase had begun to RIPPLE and spill on the floor.

Or that the teacups and saucers were shaking on the shelves.

THIS was a clear sign that EITHER:

1. A HUGE herd of elephants was thundering toward the Foot house.

OR

2. Wendy Wedge was on her way—and she was in a VERY **BAD** mood.

(Take a WILD guess which one it was.)

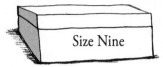

Size Nine

"GOT IT!" Ivor shouted. **"Cloud shoes, drawing shoes, sandwich shoes, bird shoes, fish, cloud, cloud, fish, fish, book."**

Nothing happened. **"For goodness' SAKE, think . . ."** he mumbled to himself.

"Cloud shoes, sandwich shoes, fish shoes, cloud, cloud, fish, fish, bird shoes, drawing shoes, book, and THEN book. I always forget the second book."

This time it worked.

The table shuddered and very slowly began to split into two. Ivor stood back and watched, willing the table to open faster.

"Come onnnnn."

The shelves inside were stuffed full
of tiny boxes filled with buttons, bolts, beads, flowers,
wires, ribbons, metal springs, miniature trees, toy animals,
and all kinds of weird and wonderful bits and pieces.

 Ivor ran his hand up and down a shelf,
then stopped at a plain-looking wooden
shoebox with a lock on the side.

"That's a good sign—it's here."

Ivor breathed a sigh of relief as he looked around for the
key. He held the box with one hand, and the lid DROPPED
off and two plain-looking shoes fell onto the floor.

"Uh-oh . . . That's NOT a good sign," Ivor said to
himself, realizing the shoebox was already UNLOCKED.

He picked up the shoes and looked them over. They seemed to be fine aside from a speck of red paint on one side. Ivor touched the paint with his finger; it was still wet.

WHERE had the paint come from?

There wasn't time to think, as the water from the vase in the kitchen was already splashing over the sides. And the teacups and saucers were RATTLING together like crazy.

Ivor looked up.

"I need to get this table shut

RIGHT NOW!"

He had to act FAST.

Ivor put the shoes away and rushed back up the ladder to close everything.

"Stay calm and everything will be just fine.* You can DO this. There's no need to panic," Ivor muttered to himself.

*Foot note: Everything was not going to be fine . . .

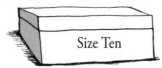

Size Ten

Thud . . .

Thud . . . Thud . . .

THUD!

The footsteps were heading toward Ivor's house, and

he could hear dogs BARKING too. The color DRAINED

from Ivor's face as he tried once again to press the tiles

down in the RIGHT order.

"Come on. Please WORK!" he muttered, now

definitely panicking.

"Think, THINK!"

The glasses on the shelves clanged together, and the

ground began to SHAKE. ALL his shoemaking secrets

WERE RIGHT THERE for anyone to SEE!

"Deep breaths . . ."

Ivor KEPT pressing

the tiles, but the table

still wasn't closing.

THUD
THUD
THUD!

The footsteps came to a HALT right OUTSIDE Ivor's front

door . . . and then everything went quiet. (But not for long.)

The door started to RATTLE, and then there was a

LOUD **KNOCK**

KNOCK

KNOCK

KNOCKING.

Ivor could hear the dogs

GROWLING too.

He shouted as loudly and calmly as he could,

"I'm on my way! Won't be long!"

KNOCK! KNOCK! KNOCK! KNOCK!

"Be with you in a minute!"

The whole front door shook as someone started

RATTLING the handle.

"HOLD ON, I'll be RIGHT WITH YOU!"

Ivor shouted, frantically stabbing the squares with his finger.

"Yes, that's it!"

The table began to MOVE, and the sides drew together slowly.

CLICK. AT LAST! The table looked like a table again.

"Calm down . . . deep breaths," Ivor told himself as he took one last look around.

"I'm HERE!" he called, rushing to the door.

"I'm on my way! Here I come! I AM—"

Just as an

ENORMOUS

METAL

WEDGE

SHOE

kicked open the door!

CLONK!

The unmistakable silhouette of Wendy Wedge stood

in the doorway. With her huge shoulder pads and thick

belt pulled in tight at the waist, Wendy cast a triangular

shadow all the way into the house. She paused for effect

(and also all that knocking had made her out of breath).

Her dogs, Left and Right, prowled and growled around her uncomfortable-looking metal wedges. Wendy STOMPED in, making everything around her shake even more.

"Wendy! What a lovely surprise. I had no idea you were coming!" Ivor said, wiping his forehead.

"What took you so long? I had to let myself in," she said, looking around suspiciously.

"I noticed. Sorry for the delay, I was—"

"WHAT were you doing?" Wendy demanded to know.

"I was . . . washing—"

Wendy interrupted him again. **"Washing?"**

Ivor's mind went blank, so he said the first thing that

popped into his head.

"Yes—a beet."

"A beet?" she repeated.

"I . . . like very . . . clean vegetables," he found himself telling her.

Wendy just stared at him, unblinkingly, like a snake about to attack.

"What can I do for you, Ms. Wedge? Is everything

okay?" Ivor said, trying to sound relaxed.

"NO, Ivor, everything is NOT okay," Wendy replied.

She thumped past him into the kitchen.

Clump. Clump. Clump. Clump.

Wendy walked up and down, until one of the dogs got

in her way and she stumbled.

"You two, wait over there and keep watch,"

Wendy ordered Left and Right.

Ivor walked past them, and they

growled. "Nice doggies," he whispered.

Ivor could usually tell what mood Wendy was in from

the shoes she was wearing. Today she was VERY:

ANNOYED,

CRANKY, and

ANGRY.

(But not necessarily in that order.)

Wendy caught Ivor staring at her feet.

 "Looking at something, Ivor?"

"Just admiring your shoes, Ms. Wedge. You do have a wonderful collection."

"That's true. I have the finest WEDGES in the world." Wendy smiled, but not in a good way.

"Although, Ivor, there is ONE pair of SHOES that I would very much like to ADD to my collection. Any idea what they could be?" Wendy narrowed her eyes until they disappeared into her face like straight little lines.

"Oh, that's a tough one," Ivor said, smiling cheerily, which was a mistake. "I'd say lovely, soft, comfy shoes? Something like a slip—"

Wendy leaned into Ivor's face.

← Furious face

"Is that your idea of a JOKE, Ivor? Slip—

I can't even SAY the word.*

THOSE SHOES
are ILLEGAL."

She thumped her foot down so hard, the dogs bounced

off the ground.

"Are they really, Ms. Wedge?" Ivor said. This was

NEWS to him.

*Foot note: The word is "slippers," in case you were wondering.

Wendy turned her back on Ivor, then STOMPED
toward the kitchen. She paused at the table and
began drumming her fingers on the shoe tiles.

"NO, Ivor. The ONE pair of shoes that I don't
have in my collection begins with an **F.**"

Ivor was starting to sweat.

"Shoes beginning with F? LET me guess: Flippers?
Flip-flops? FURRY shoes?"

"FLYING SHOES, IVOR! I don't yet have
a pair of FLYING SHOES. But somebody ELSE in
Wedge Town DOES!"

Wendy *GLARED* at him.

Ivor tried to look shocked. **"REALLY? A pair of shoes that can fly is IMPOSSIBLE, right?"**

"Oh, they exist, Ivor, and I'm GOING to find out WHO has them, even if I have to search every house in Wedge Town."

"Don't you mean SHOE TOWN, Ms. Wedge?" Ivor asked.

"NOT anymore. I think Wedge Town has a certain ring to it, don't you agree?"

(Ivor didn't.)

"We've all tried to make flying shoes for you many times, Ms. Wedge," he reminded her. **"And no one has succeeded."**

"WELL, SOMEONE HAS SUCCEEDED! And is trying to keep them a secret," she snarled. **"AND I NEED THOSE FLYING SHOES TO WIN THE GOLDEN SHOE AWARD!"**

Wendy pointed an accusing finger at Ivor.

"YOU used to make shoes with gadgets, didn't you? In that little shop you used to run."

"Not really—they were just plain old boring shoes . . . nothing like the AMAZING ones we—I mean, YOU—create at World of Wedge," Ivor added quickly. But Wendy wasn't convinced.

"Hmmmmmm." Wendy began to look around his kitchen. She stopped to pick up a picture frame.

"Oh, look," she said. "Your beautiful wife. Dear Sally Sandal. How we miss her. Such a terrible tragedy—to die from a teeny-weeny little snakebite."

Ivor took the picture from Wendy and carefully put it back. "Yes," he said quietly. "We all miss her very much."

"It's hard raising children on your own," Wendy said. "I know that only too well. And very difficult keeping them out of trouble. YOUR TWO, for instance. Did you know they were sent home from school EARLY today?"

"No, I didn't know that," Ivor said.

Wendy's voice grew softer and more menacing.

"Walter told me ALL about it. They had EXTRA gadgets in their school WOW shoes. Which is SERIOUSLY breaking the RULES."

Ivor gulped. "You know what kids are like; they were probably just showing off. I'll talk to them later, Ms. Wedge."

"NO, I'll talk to them RIGHT NOW. And I think I'll ask them about the FLYING shoes too. It's quite the coincidence, isn't it?"

"They don't know anything about the flying shoes and neither do I." Ivor stood up and tried to sound calm. "Maybe whoever saw them made a mistake?"

"Are you calling my son a LIAR?" Wendy asked.

"No, no, absolutely not, Ms. Wedge."

"Because my Walter NEVER lies. He said a person dropped RED PAINT all over him and then flew OFF!"

"Really? That's terrible. Is Walter okay?" Ivor asked her.

She shrugged. "He's still slightly red and wasn't happy about having to take a bath. But the POINT IS, Ivor . . ."

Wendy THUMPED the mosaic table with her fist. She hit it SO hard a crack appeared in the middle. Ivor held his breath.

"SOMEONE in

WEDGE TOWN . . ."

THUMP

"HAS GOT FLYING SHOES!"

THUMP

"AND I MUST HAVE

THEM!"

THUMP

"I *HAVE* **TO WIN . . ."**

THUMP

"THE

GOLDEN . . ."

THUMP

"SHOE

AWARD."

THUMP!

On the LAST ***thump***, the table creaked. And then,

to Ivor's horror, it started opening ever so slightly.

"NO!" Ivor shouted.

"What do you mean, NO?" Wendy said.

 She looked confused. "No" wasn't a

word she heard very often.

"Sorry, I just meant . . . the table's delicate,

Ms. Wedge. You don't want to hurt your hand if a tile

breaks."

Wendy stared at Ivor.

"Do you remember signing a contract, Ivor?"

(How could he forget?)

The contract was SUPER LONG with a LOT of conditions written in teeny-tiny writing.

SIGN HERE
Ivor Foot

"I do, Ms. Wedge. It was very long with a lot of teeny-tiny writing on it that was extremely hard to read."

"Well, I can tell you what it said. ALL the shoes you have ever made in your whole entire LIFE now belong to World of Wedge—that's me. Not 'some shoes,' Ivor. ALL OF THEM."

Ivor kept quiet.

"And I would HATE for you to lose your job and everything you own. After all, who would look after your children?" Wendy began to trace a long, pointy finger over the painted shoes tiles again, tapping them in a way that made Ivor nervous. He could see the gap in the table that all her THUMPING had opened up.

"I DESERVE to win **THE GOLDEN SHOE AWARD**, don't you think? This year I WILL win it. And DO YOU know HOW that's going to happen, IVOR?"

"**You bribed all the judges?**" Ivor guessed.

"NO—BY ENTERING WITH FLYING SHOES!" Wendy

shouted, and stamped her foot again. A small HATCH opened from the back of her wedge, and a metal claw SPRANG out.

"**Not now!**" Wendy snapped, and it popped back in.

Her STEELY eyes spotted the vase of flowers that Ivor had forgotten to put back on the table. **"Why are they on the floor?"** she asked.

"I was about to give them more water," he tried to explain.

Wendy picked them up and sniffed them.

"Ugh, revolting! **Horrible dead weeds. THROW THEM OUT!"**

"Ruby and Bear picked them for me. They're good kids, Wendy," Ivor told her.

"We'll see about that. Let's go and have that talk with them, shall we?" Wendy gave Ivor a terrifying smile.

"But, Ms. Wedge . . . they're . . ."

Before he could say anything else, Wendy STOMPED OFF down the hall.

It wasn't hard to find their room in such a small house. Wendy stopped outside and SHOUTED . . .

"Ruby! Bear! It's your favorite aunty Wendy here! I'm coming in to SAY HELLO!"

She glanced at Ivor.

"Why are they HIDING from me?"

"They're not, they're just . . ."

Wendy put on a horrible

sickly sweet voice.

"I KNOW you're in THERE! READY OR NOT, HERE I COME!"

She SLID OPEN the door and went in.

"Ms. Wedge, I was trying to tell you, they're . . .

NOT . . ."** Ivor sputtered.

"**. . . FEELING VERY WELL,**" he finished.

Ruby and Bear were standing there. They were

were both covered in

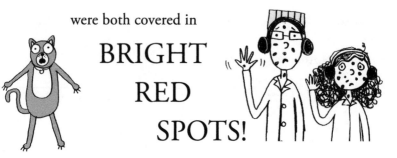

BRIGHT
RED
SPOTS!

They looked up and WAVED weakly.

Wendy jumped back in horror. She hated any kind

of illness almost as much as she hated slippers.

"**We're not feeling great, so we got into our pajamas,**"

Ruby said in a really soft voice.

"**We're listening to soothing music,**" Bear added in

a scratchy voice, pointing to their headphones. Ivor was

almost as surprised as Wendy to see them at HOME with

spots all over their faces. When had they gotten back?

"**Oh no, you POOR things!**" he said as Wendy

continued to edge away.

Ruby and Bear came closer.

"The spots just came UP. Do you want to see?" Ruby

asked Wendy, who was

already FREAKING out.

"STAY where you are—don't come NEAR me!" Wendy shouted, then turned to Ivor.

"Why didn't you tell me they were SICK, Ivor? Is it contagious? What do they have? WHY did you let me in the HOUSE if you knew they were covered in SPOTS?!"

"I didn't really have a choice," Ivor reminded her.

"KEEP THEM AWAY FROM ME."

Wendy looked down to see Shoo

the cat hiding behind her wedges.

She bent down and GRABBED Shoo, then held her

up as a shield. **"I'm LEAVING NOW, BUT I KNOW**

you're HIDING SOMETHING.

I WANT those FLYING shoes!"

Wendy told him, still holding

Shoo, who hissed at her.

"You know something too,

I bet," Wendy hissed back at

Shoo. **"Nice fur. You'd make a lovely pair of kitten**

heels for me!" She turned to Ivor. **"Just remember—I'll**

be WATCHING you, your spotty children, and your

CUTE little kitty."

"PUT Shoo DOWN! You're scaring her,"

Ruby said angrily.

"DON'T come any CLOSER." Wendy began

to BACK away, still holding Shoo up for

protection. The dogs ran over, BARKING like

CRAZY as Shoo scrambled onto Wendy's shoulders

to escape.

Wendy screamed, **"GET OFF ME!"** and Shoo

obeyed, leaping off, sending Wendy

wobbling backward.

She swung her arms

around wildly, trying

not to fall.

"WEDGES CONNECT! NOW!" Wendy

SHRIEKED, and a large metal claw appeared from the

back of each WEDGE to keep her upright.

"Control yourselves, Left and Right!" Wendy

shouted as she wobbled out the door.

Ivor quickly SLAMMED it shut behind her, then took

a BIG deep BREATH IN.

"Did you see her face?"

Ruby laughed.

"Her arms," Bear joined in,

doing an impression of Wendy falling.

Ivor double locked the door, then

turned to the kids with a very SERIOUS look.

"Well, you've both made a quick recovery,"

he said suspiciously, rubbing one of the

spots on Bear's cheek with his finger.

It smeared into a splodge.

"Red paint?" he asked.

"Maybe . . ." Ruby whispered.

"We had to do something, Dad! It was an emergency!"

Bear explained.

Ivor took out the feather he had found earlier and held

it up in front of them.

"This was in your room. Any idea where it came from?" he asked.

"A bird?" said Bear.

"OR a duck?" Ruby added.

"A duck IS a bird," Bear pointed out.

"You didn't say what kind of bird, though—and ducks can be white, so it could be from a duck. Or a pigeon . . ." Ruby said.

Ivor shook his head.

"Come on, you two—I think we need to have a little chat. After you've washed off those fake spots," he said, looking at them sternly.

"You won't be angry, will you, Dad?" Ruby asked anxiously.

"Clean up first, then you can tell me **everything.**"*

*Foot note: There was a LOT to tell.

116

Shoo gets comfy.

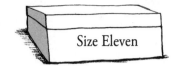

Size Eleven

"You did WHAT?"

Ivor could hardly believe what he was hearing.

"Don't worry, Dad, no one saw us," Ruby said.

"We made sure of that," Bear added.

"Let me get this straight. You TOOK my flying shoes from my workshop. THEN you used them to FLY to the BRAND-NEW Wedge Town sign and paint a heart over it?"

The kids nodded. **"It looks so much better now, Dad. You should see it,"** Ruby told him.

KEY!

Ivor shook his head. **"HOW did you even know where to FIND the shoes? I can't hide anything from you two, can I?"**

"You could hide beets," said Ruby.

"We'd NEVER look for THAT."

"What's wrong with beets?" Dad sounded slightly

confused.

"They taste like dirt!" Ruby made a face.

"How do YOU know what dirt tastes like?"

Bear asked.

"I had some on a carrot once by accident, when I

was little," Ruby told Bear. **"It tastes kind of earthy,**

like beets. Yuck."

"Enough about BEETS! Let's get back to what

you've both been up to?" Dad asked.

Ruby and Bear took deep breaths and started to tell

Dad ALL about Walter Wedge.

(Yes, HIM . . .)

"First of all, I found out that Walter Wedge had been moved to MY class at school," Bear said. "He was sitting right next to me."

"Oh dear . . ." Dad muttered.

"He pushed past us outside, like he was SO special," Ruby added.

"Sounds like Walter Wedge. What happened next?" Dad wanted to know.

"He brought a BIG bag of FAKE spiders and bugs in to play pranks on me and everyone else. Walter put a whoopie cushion on my seat and then chucked a fake spider at Freddie Flat," Bear said.

"Did Walter get in trouble?" Dad asked.

"No way. Teachers aren't ALLOWED to yell at Walter." Bear sighed.

"But get this, Dad—Bear hid all of Walter's pranks." Ruby sounded proud of her brother.

"Walter wasn't happy. But I was going to give them back eventually," Bear said.

"Nice one!" Ruby high-fived him.

"It put Walter in a VERY bad mood. He was super sulky and refused to participate in gym class. Walter got a note from his mother that EXCUSES him from pretty much EVERYTHING he doesn't want to do," Bear said.

"*I'd* like one of *those*." Ruby smiled.

"Nice try, Ruby. Go on, Bear,"

Dad said with a chuckle.

Uh-oh.

"So, Miss Mule suggested he go to the library if he wanted to. Only he didn't. He waited until we were all

in GYM, then SEARCHED the class for the fake bugs and FOUND them in my desk. So he knew it was me. Then he put them all in our shoes and socks as a nice surprise."

Dad sighed. **"Sounds like Walter."**

"And that's when he must have noticed that MY shoes had EXTRA gadgets inside—thanks to you, Dad. They are great, by the way."

"Thanks, Bear," Dad said.

"He went straight to Mr. Moccasin and showed him. Then Mr. Moccasin called me and Ruby into his office. Walter was there smiling at us in a 'serves you right' kind of way."

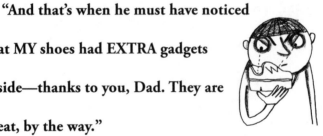

"He told Mr. Moccasin that his MOTHER was going to hear all about our shoes and we should be given a VERY BIG punishment.

"THEN he suggested lots of extra homework for a YEAR, cleaning everyone's shoes, AND detention too," Bear explained.

"Hey! I was the one who broke the shoe rules—not you two. I'm going to call Mr. Moccasin right now and explain," Dad interrupted.

"It's fine, Dad," Ruby said. "Mr. Moccasin sent Walter off, then told us to go home early and to never wear the shoes again. And that was it! No punishment!"

"Good for Mr. Moccasin!" Dad said, pleased and relieved.

"We didn't want to get YOU in trouble, Dad. So I told him it was US who changed the shoes," Bear said.

"Did he believe you?"

"He was impressed and told us to keep INVENTING—just not on our WOW school shoes," Bear said.

"Can we get to the part where you STOLE my flying shoes now?" Dad asked.

"So, we were on our way home early and we stopped in to see Bert in his shoe shop. He was busy painting protest signs," said Bear.

"Good old Bert," Dad told them. "His is the only shoe shop in town that's NOT owned by Wendy Wedge."

"Bert told us she wants to close down his shop," said Ruby.

"Ah."

"So we joined in and painted our own signs!"

Dad sighed. "Of course you did."

"Mine was the best. It said:

Don't BE SHOE-PID.
KEEP BERT'S SHOP OPEN!"

she added.

"He's got some fancy new shoe styles in his shop, Dad—you should see them," Bear said excitedly. "And he knows a lot of good stories about what **SHOE TOWN** USED to be like, before Wendy Wedge took over. He showed us photos of you and Mom when you were younger."

"With bad hair, Dad," Ruby told him.

"Hey—that was a good look back then," Ivor protested.

They both shook their heads. "No, Dad, it really wasn't."

"Okay, so you went to Bert's, painted some protest signs, and then what did you do?"

"We left the shop and spotted Mr. Creeper with a group of Wedge workers putting up the NEW Wedge Town sign," Ruby told Dad. "LIKE there aren't ENOUGH things NAMED after her already?"

"Why does Wendy get to put her NAME all over OUR town?" Bear wondered.

"Because SHE owns most of it," Dad explained sadly.

"Well, that's not fair! Anyway, we're both looking up at the SIGN and we decide **SHOE TOWN** is a MUCH better name than WEDGE TOWN. And that's when I had the BEST IDEA EVER!" said Ruby.

"We'd BORROW the flying shoes, FLY up to the sign, and paint over it!" Bear said.

"HOW did you even know where my flying shoes were kept?" Dad wanted to know.

"Ummm . . . You won't get mad?" Bear asked.

"I'll try not to."

"Well, I saw you open up the kitchen table. I was hiding behind the bookshelf," Bear told him.

"HEY, that's MY spot!" Ruby said.

"But how did you know the code? I can't even remember it most of the time," Dad asked.

"I have a good memory. I saw you do it once—and that was enough." Bear tapped his head.

Dad began to look nervous.

"We were very careful with the shoes, Dad, I promise," Ruby assured him before continuing. "THEN, as we were leaving the house, Mrs. Court suddenly appeared, wondering why we weren't in school."

"She MUST have seen the shoes," Dad said.

"No, but she asked about the red paint we were carrying. I said it was for a school project, and we'd come home to collect it," Ruby told Dad.

"Good thinking, Ruby."

"I'm not sure she believed us, though. But then Shoo started purring all around her walking stick. That distracted her, so we snuck off," Ruby explained.

"By the time we'd got to the sign, there was no one around. So I put on the shoes, and used the special-adjustment panel for different-sized feet. That was a VERY smart thing you added, Dad."

"I try my best," Dad said, blushing proudly.

"Then I gave Ruby a piggyback while she held on to the paint."

"And I said, loud and clear, 'Shoes UP,'" Ruby added.

"We lifted off the ground, so I said it again—'SHOES UP!'—and suddenly, we were as tall as the sign. It was AMAZING, Dad!"

"All Ruby had to do was paint a heart over the 'DGE' quickly, then she wrote 'SHOE' and I kept us steady," Bear continued.

"It says WE HEART **SHOE TOWN**, and looks much better," Ruby said proudly.

"It was all going really well when the one person we DIDN'T want to see, Walter Wedge, started heading our way."

Dad looked a little pale as Ruby picked up the story.

"We quickly FLEW behind a tree and hovered. Walter SPOTTED the sign—and he wasn't HAPPY . . ."

"That's when we lost control of the shoes. They SUDDENLY SWAYED to the left and then to the right and the PAINT spilled . . ." Bear paused.

"ONTO WALTER," Ruby said, trying not to smile.

"Of ALL the places it COULD have landed, it HAD to be ON Wendy's SON," Dad said, knowing this was not good at all.

"It took a moment for it to sink in," Bear said.

"The paint?" Dad asked.

"No—where the paint had come from. Walter looked all confused."

"And all red too . . ." Ruby added.

"We tried to fly back to the house but our flying was WOBBLY. We were ALL over the place!"

"HOW did no one see you?" Dad wondered.

"We were smart, Dad. We tried to fly low and Bear hid us really well behind a TREE," said Ruby reassuringly.

"Then we rushed home to put the shoes BACK, but you were already in the house," Bear told him. "We had to figure out how to get past you."

"But HOW?" asked Dad. "I would have seen you."

"Oh, this part's good," said Ruby.

"Ruby took a letter from our mailbox and slipped it through Mrs. Court's door," explained Bear.

"YES—and then she came around with it," Dad said. "THAT'S when you two snuck in." Ruby and Bear nodded.

"Mrs. Court's SO nosy, we knew she wouldn't just GIVE it back," Bear said. "And we knew she'd keep you chatting for ages."

"We climbed through the window while you talked. Bear put the shoes back in the box and CLOSED the table."

"The perfect crime," said Dad, sighing. "I suppose I should be impressed."

"Then after SHE left we heard all that BANGING on the door," Bear continued.

"WE knew that Walter would have blabbed. We had to think FAST! That's when we put the red paint on our faces. We knew that would do the trick. Wendy hates spots," Bear said, and high-fived Ruby.

Dad looked at them both. "Is that it? Nothing more to add?"

Ruby and Bear shook their heads.

"What if you'd been caught? What if you had gotten hurt?" Dad worried.

"We're FINE, AND the shoes are THE BEST! YOU should enter **THE GOLDEN SHOE AWARDS**, Dad! You'd win it for sure!" Ruby exclaimed.

"You totally would!" Bear agreed.

"I can't," said Dad. **"I signed a contract with World of Wedge. Every shoe I made, now and in the past, belongs to Wendy."**

"But you didn't make the shoes," Bear said slowly. **"Mom did. So you can enter them?"**

Dad shook his head. **"It's too risky. I can't prove that was Mom. Imagine if Wendy took them away? Your mom would hate that. She'd never forgive me."**

"But, Dad, last night I heard you tell Shoo that Mom would be SO proud if you won **THE GOLDEN SHOE AWARD**," Ruby reminded him.

"I was tired, Ruby. I'd be out of a job if that

happened."

"You could work with

Bert Brogue, just like

the old days. If you were

making flying shoes, everyone would buy them, and he

could keep his shop open with all the NEW customers.

You wouldn't need Wendy Wedge anymore."

Dad stood up. **"It's not going to happen."** He sighed.

"Wendy has plans to CLOSE DOWN Bert's shop. She'll

find a way to do it somehow. But she CAN'T take your

mom's shoes too. So promise me—NO more flying shoe

trips?"

Bear and Ruby mumbled a sort of yes.

"Pinkie promise?" Dad asked, holding his finger out.

All three of them linked their little fingers together and

made a pact.

"Pinkie promise."

Dad frowned. **"Can anyone hear a weird buzzing noise?"**

"Probably my stomach rumbling," Ruby suggested. **"I'm really hungry. It's all that flying."**

"Me too," said Bear. **"What's for dinner?"**

"Nothing with beets, I hope," Ruby told Bear, who made a face.

While the Foot family was busy making promises and talking about dinner, the tall shadowy figure of Mr. Creeper was lurking around outside. And he had heard EVERYTHING.

Size Twelve

Mr. Creeper was Wendy's loyal and long-suffering assistant. Wendy trusted Mr. Creeper, but it didn't stop her from being mean to him. (Like she was to most people.) So why did Mr. Creeper keep working there?

Good question.

Wendy had always promised him a **MIGHTY BIG** promotion. **"You'll be VERY important. Obviously not AS important as ME, but then who is?"**

Mr. Creeper kept hoping that Wendy would keep her promise. But it hadn't happened yet.

Wendy had STOMPED away from the Foots' house, and with every step, she became EVEN MORE convinced that Ivor Foot and his annoying children KNEW something about the flying shoes.

So she DEMANDED that Mr. Creeper GO back

to the **Shoebox neighborhood.** **"Those fiendish FOOTS**

are up to something, I know it. Find the EVIDENCE or,

even better, find the flying shoes."

"And if they're not there?" Mr. Creeper had asked,

which made Wendy have a huge MELTDOWN.

"JUST GET ME THE FRYING SHOES!"

This confused Mr. Creeper. **"FRYING shoes?"** he'd

asked.

"Don't be RIDICULOUS.
I WANT those
FLYING SHOES!"

Wendy's face was as RED as a strawberry.

Mr. Creeper crept away as fast as he could.

He'd quickly thought of a plan (in between thinking

about cookies . . .). Mr. Creeper headed straight to the

WOW workshop and then to buy a cookie tin.

All the WEDGE creations for tomorrow's

GOLDEN SHOE AWARDS were kept there.

(The workshop, not the cookie tin.)

He'd just borrow the impressive CAMERA WEDGES that Ivor Foot had been working on. Did he feel guilty about STEALING Ivor's shoes?

No, he did not.

"This is a SHOEmergency,"* Mr. Creeper said to himself, with a mouthful of chocolate chips.

*Foot note: An emergency—but for shoes.

Size Thirteen

Mr. Creeper changed out of his own shoes (which were a little smelly), lifted the temperature-controlled glass dome off Ivor's camera wedges, and put them on. Then he activated the AUTOMATIC shoe adjuster so the wedges would fit his own feet perfectly.

(For a tall man, Mr. Creeper had very tiny toes.)

Next he clipped the control panel onto his wrist and

said, **"TURN. WEDGES. ON."**

Nothing happened.

He repeated it again and again using

different voices, but none of them worked.

"So annoying . . ." he mumbled. Then he spotted what

looked like an instruction pamphlet, open to the page that

said . . .

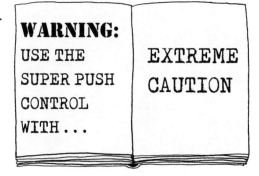

WARNING:
USE THE
SUPER PUSH
CONTROL
WITH . . .

EXTREME
CAUTION

"Noted . . ."

Mr. Creeper said, storing it in his memory.

He flicked through the booklet until he found a page that

said

TECHNICAL PROBLEMS.

"This is what I need," he muttered.

"If the voice control isn't responding, try

turning it OFF and then ON again."

Which seemed to do the trick.

The WEDGES sprang to life.

Mr. Creeper glanced at his reflection

in the window. **"Not bad . . ."** He nodded

to himself in approval.

"Not bad at all."

Now all set with the
camera wedges on his feet,
he made his way back to the
Foots' house. He strode past the two
guards at the WOW door, and a quick
wave of his ID lifted the gate up.

"You haven't seen me," Mr. Creeper
hissed at them. **"And you definitely
haven't seen me wearing these
WEDGES."**

Mr. Creeper crept down to the
Shoebox neighborhood, glancing
around to make sure no one was
watching, before darting behind a
particularly WIDE TREE right
outside the Foots' house.

He then tapped the screen on his wrist and, using the voice control, whispered, **"RAISE wedges UP,"** to get a better view.

Mr. Creeper could see the family sitting around the table talking.

"Perfect." He smiled menacingly. Then he stretched out his RIGHT foot and whispered, **"Release camera."**

From a compartment in his heel, a long metal arm slowly uncurled from his shoe. It slithered along the ground, and then crept up the side of the house until it was pointed directly at the Foots' window.

Mr. Creeper checked the screen on his wrist to get a good clear picture.

"Focus and record."

The sound was a bit muffled at first, but he could distinctly make out some kind of . . . purrrring, just before the whole screen went DARK.

"Camera," he whispered desperately. **"Left, down, focus. FOCUS."**

Suddenly, TWO BRIGHT EYES ZOOMED into view and were **STARING** right at him.

"Out of the way—hey! Stupid CAT!" He tried moving the camera, but all he could see was its TAIL swishing back and forth.

Finally, Mr. Creeper managed to get high enough so the cat couldn't block his view, just in time to HEAR Ivor say TWO VERY IMPORTANT WORDS:

"FLYING SHOES."

Mr. Creeper listened and listened and smiled an evil smile.

"YES! Thank you, Ivor Foot. I heard you loud and clear—and so will everyone else now." HE HAD EVIDENCE! Mr. Creeper would WAVE Ivor's contract around to remind him what he'd agreed to, the **shoe police** could be his backup and look tough, and Wendy could take what was rightfully hers: the flying shoes.

It was time to get back. Wendy would be thrilled and CONGRATULATE him—and MAYBE give him that long-awaited promotion! He deserved it.

Mr. Creeper was imagining himself sitting in a new office, with NEW shoes and his feet up on the desk, when

PING!

SOMETHING stung him on the NECK.

"Ow!" It felt like a wasp sting.

There was another *PING* that HIT something above his HEAD.

"I hate wasps," he said, looking around. It was time to get out of here. Mr. Creeper whispered into his wrist control, **"Bring camera back."**

It slid down the wall and was snaking toward him when it STOPPED with a jolt. The camera was caught on something.

"What now?" repeated Mr. Creeper.

"Camera back. NOT YOU again."

He sighed when he saw what it was.

Shoo had pounced on the camera like it was a MOUSE.

"Water jet ON," Mr. Creeper said, and watched Shoo get soaked, then JUMP up and let go.

"Good. Now bring camera back!"

It slithered across the ground, folding inside his wedge heel with a satisfying click.

"Phew," he sighed. But then something began to $BUZZ$ around his head. It was another WASP. He tilted his foot upright to check that the camera was back in place. It was time to leave.

"Get lost!" he murmured under his breath, and SWIPED at it with his hand.

Then *PING!*

He'd gotten stung on both sides

of his neck. Mr. Creeper smacked his

neck to try to stop the wasp.

PING!

It got him on his arm next.

PING! Then his CHEEK.

PING! He slapped his own

face to get rid of the wasp, but

it landed on his wrist control.

After shaking it a few times, Mr.

Creeper got ANGRY and BASHED

the controls over and over again

with his other hand. **"Take**

THAT!" he hissed, before

accidentally HITTING the

SUPER
PUSH-UP
CONTROL
button.

The wedges made a weird noise that didn't sound good.

"Oh no," he whispered, but it was too late.

They tipped him BACK and turned to maximum **POWER,**

then

SHOT

him UP

in the

air

like

a

cork

from

a

bottle.

Mr. Creeper reached out for the nearest branch and held on as tight as he could. Then he looked up and saw a wasp nest RIGHT NEXT TO HIS HANDS! **"Uh-oh!"** He let go and fell to the ground with a THUD. **"Stupid wasps,"** Mr. Creeper grumbled, and dusted himself off. Checking to make sure the CAMERA wedges were still working, he put them back on and vowed to NEVER press the super push-up control button again.

"Lucky escape. Now off to tell Wendy the GOOD news," he said . . . just as the wasp nest CRASHED DOWN at his feet and the angry wasps SWARMED OUT all over him.

Mr. Creeper RAN as fast as he could to try to shake

the WASPS off. He LEAPED over the WOW barrier like

an Olympic hurdler. The guards screamed,

"STOP! INTRUDER!"

and let the dogs loose.

"It's ME! It's ME!" Mr. Creeper shouted.

He stumbled into

the W-shaped

fountain, taking cover

under the waterfall

to SAVE himself, forgetting all

about the high-tech camera wedges

he still had on his feet.

(No, the shoes were not waterproof.)

Mr. Creeper stayed there until the wasps left and the

guards called off the dogs.

On the upside, things could only get better for

Mr. Creeper.*

*Foot note: although not by much.

Size Fourteen

It was early morning when Walter came to see Wendy, who was sitting at her dressing table and putting on makeup.

"Walter, my little WEDGE, are you all right? You look a tiny bit . . . PINK? It's not a rash, is it?" Wendy asked, putting on her fake eyelashes and leaning away (just in case he was contagious).

"No!" Walter snapped. **"It's still the RED PAINT! I can't get it off. I've had TWO baths and I HATE bathing! You have to find out who did this to me, Mom."**

"Poor Walty, I PROMISE we'll find the culprits. I already have my suspicions," Wendy assured him.

"GOOD, because they need to be punished. I'll put itching powder in their socks and set the DOGS on them!" Walter hissed, eager for revenge.

"Of course you will. Those weasels RUINED my Wedge Town sign too," Wendy told him.

Wendy held up the EYEBROW chart next to her face.

What SHAPE for today?

ANGRY?

SURPRISED?

FIERCE?

She settled on

FIERCE and began to draw them on as Walter watched.

"TODAY is VERY important, Walter," she explained.

"My WEDGE workers are presenting their shoe

creations to me, and they'd better be good. I HAVE to

win THE GOLDEN SHOE AWARD this year.

I'll make sure NO one laughs at me again." She stopped,

noticing that Walter was looking confused.

"What's wrong? Too fierce?" Wendy asked.

"Too WONKY. A little like

a wobbly worm, Mom,"

Walter pointed out.

(Not the look Wendy was going for.)

155

She wiped them off and quickly redrew them.

"What about MY face?" Walter asked, feeling frustrated.

"You look GORGEOUS—just like me, only pinker and with less fabulous eyebrows. The paint will come off . . . eventually," Wendy reassured him.

"Well, I'm not taking another bath—EVER!" Walter said stubbornly.

Wendy ignored his comment and looked around impatiently for Mr. Creeper.

"Where is that man? He SHOULD be here by now with important NEWS for me. What's taking him so long?"

Wendy was getting mad. She picked up the phone.

"FIND Mr. Creeper and tell him to get here now," she yelled at a minion. As she slammed down the phone, there was a KNOCK at the door.

"About TIME!" Wendy shouted as the door began to slowly open.

In came a limping, shuffling figure covered in bandages and making a terrible sound.

Wendy looked frightened (and her newly drawn EYEBROWS made her look even MORE frightened) as the person got closer. **"MOM, who's that?"** Walter shouted.

"Stay back!" Wendy yelled at the figure. But it kept coming closer, slowly taking off more and more bandages to speak. **"ONE step nearer and I'm calling the DOGS! LEFT and RIGHT—SEIZE them!"** Wendy screamed. But the person kept coming.

So Wendy protected herself the ONLY way she knew how.

By **SHOVING** Walter in front of her.

"It's only meeeeee . . ." the intruder

managed to say before

the dogs ran in GROWLING

and CHOMPED down on

his legs.

"AGGGHH! Noooooh . . . it's ME!

Mr. Creeper!" he SQUEALED.

"For goodness' sake, Mr. Creeper, WHAT ARE you

doing?" Wendy asked furiously as she finally

  recognized him.

"Put him down."

Reluctantly, Left and Right let go of his legs.

"You look like a MESS! And, much more

importantly, DO you HAVE MY flying shoes?"

"I've GOT the proof here that Ivor Foot DOES have

them." Mr. Creeper held up the camera wedges, now

busted and covered in seaweed.

"WHAT on EARTH happened?" Wendy asked.

"I got really badly stung by . . ."

Mr. Creeper started to say.

"**NO.** I'm not interested in YOU."

(Wendy didn't do sympathy.)

"Oh, of course you're not. You were right,

Ms. Wedge. Ivor broke his contract. He made

FLYING shoes and hid them from you. AND I have his

confession on video."

If Mr. Creeper was expecting to be congratulated by

Wendy, it didn't happen.

"ARE YOU an IDIOT?" Wendy asked, seething with

anger. "I don't want to see PICTURES; I want the

REAL DEAL."

"Absolutely. WHAT was I thinking? I'll call the

SHOE POLICE RIGHT NOW to search the house,"

Mr. Creeper said quickly, frantically trying to make

things better.

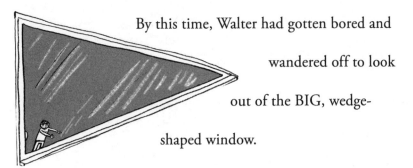

By this time, Walter had gotten bored and wandered off to look out of the BIG, wedge-shaped window.

"Look, Mom! It's the FOOTS! Let's send the dogs to get them NOW!" he shouted, pointing at Ivor, Ruby, and Bear, who were on their way to school.

Wendy glanced down. **"Good catch, Walter. Look at them skipping away, not a care in the world. The dogs can wait: I have other plans. Be patient, Walter. That FOUL FOOT FAMILY has been lying to me for all this time,"** she hissed. **"Ivor won't be going ANYWHERE until I get MY shoes. And as for his AWFUL children, I'll deal with them later."**

"WITH ITCHING POWDER!" Walter screeched. He picked up the prank he'd been saving for a special occasion.

GENIUS

"You are SO smart, Walter. Isn't he, Mr. Creeper?"

Mr. Creeper nodded as if his life depended on it.*

"Ivor will be looking for his camera wedges. I think it's time for some FUN," Wendy added, rubbing her hands together at the thought of what was to come.

"In the meantime, GET me those flying shoes, Mr. Creeper. NOTHING can be left to chance. I don't want EXCUSES—WHATEVER it takes, JUST DO IT!" Wendy told him, then tried to WINK. Which Mr. Creeper mistook for a TWITCH.

"DO YOU UNDERSTAND?" she asked him again.

Mr. Creeper tried to nod back, but his neck was in too much pain. And thanks to Walter, he was starting to ITCH in places he shouldn't.

He was NOT having a good day.

*Foot note: It did.

161

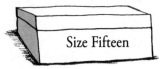

Size Fifteen

Ivor dropped the kids off at school and hurried through the gates of World of Wedge. It was the BIG shoe presentation day, and everyone would be trying to IMPRESS Wendy by demonstrating their own Wedge shoe creations.

Ivor was hoping that his camera shoes would impress Wendy so much she'd forget about the flying shoes. They might even win **THE GOLDEN SHOE AWARD**.

(It was a long shot, but Ivor had done his best.) He tried to RELAX as he joined his coworkers in the locker room.

"Morning, Parminder Platform. Big day ahead."

"Tell me about it." She smiled nervously.

"How are things, Harry Heel?

Nice beard trim, by the way."

Ivor put on his WOW white coat.

"All set for **THE GOLDEN SHOE AWARD**

presentation, Ivor?" Pauline Plimsoll asked.

"**As ready as I'll ever be.**" Ivor sighed.

"**I've heard Wendy's in a terrible mood,**" Pauline said,

lowering her voice. "**We could be in for a toe-curling day**

if she's not happy. Remember last time? She forced us

to work all night long on HER LIFT-OFF WOODEN

wedges, when we all KNEW they were too heavy to fly."

Ivor shrugged. "**Wendy doesn't listen. She's obsessed**

with winning **THE GOLDEN SHOE AWARD.**

It wasn't our fault they never took off."

"**Shhh, she might hear you,**" Pauline said, and scanned

her badge to get into the workshop. BEEP.

Next, Ivor scanned his. It didn't BEEP.

He tried again. And again. He turned to the other

workers and apologized.

"**Sorry, I'm not sure what's wrong.**"

Then a face appeared on the screen.

It was their supervisor, **Lottie Loafer.**

"Morning, Lottie. Why can't I get in? Is there a problem?" Ivor asked.

"Ms. Wedge wants you to head right to her office for the presentations today, Ivor. And Ms. Wedge says she'd BETTER be impressed. Or else."

"IMPRESSED is my middle name," Ivor said.

"Is it?"

"No, Lottie. I just make jokes when I'm nervous," he explained.

"You need better jokes," Lottie said, then disappeared off the screen.

Ivor did not have a good feeling about today.

BEEP!
BEEP!

Mr. Creeper was waiting for him outside Wendy's office. He was moving strangely and still had bandages on his face. He motioned for Ivor to wait.

"**What happened to you?**" Ivor asked.

"**Wasp nest,**" Mr. Creeper said very matter-of-factly, which put Ivor on edge.

"**Shouldn't I be getting my WEDGES ready to present with everyone else?**" Ivor asked cautiously. But Mr. Creeper just stared straight ahead and ignored him.

"**So, what DO I get to present to Ms. Wedge, then?**" Ivor tried again.

Mr. Creeper pointed to Wendy's office door.

"**Your WEDGES are already in there,**" he snapped, and scratched his foot.

"Well, that's good, then." Ivor smiled at him.

Mr. Creeper didn't smile back.

"SssssssssHHHHHHhhhhhhhhhhhhhh."

Ivor was joined by Betty Boot, who sat down next to him and raised an eyebrow in a "what's going on?" kind of way. **"Where are YOUR camera wedges?"** she whispered.

Ivor shrugged.

"In there already, apparently," he said quietly.

The rest of the WOW team arrived. They'd finished cleaning, polishing, and adjusting their SHOWCASE wedges, and now all that was left was the PRESENTATION to Wendy. Whose wedges would she like the most?

Mr. Creeper slid the door open. **"You can go in now,"** he told them.

"What happened to you?" Harry Heel asked.

"Nothing, what do you mean? I'm completely fine," Mr. Creeper told him.

"You don't look fine," Betty pointed out.

They all wheeled in the glass domes covering their various shoe creations, except for Ivor. He still couldn't see his camera wedges. *What is Wendy up to?* he wondered.

The room went dark, and purple lights began to flash on and off from behind huge glass sliding doors. The team watched as Wendy and Walter appeared in silhouette. Wendy loved a BUILDUP and never missed an opportunity to make an entrance.

They HELD their pose and waited for the music to begin.

None of this was helping Ivor feel less nervous. Betty whispered to him, **"Purple's a good color."**

"If you're a grape," he replied, and they both tried not to laugh.

"Shouldn't Walter be in shoe school?" Betty wondered.

"He's being trained for great things," Ivor told her.

"Or GRAPE things . . ." Betty laughed again.

The dogs growled at them and Mr. Creeper glared in their direction, so they stopped talking.

The doors began to slide open as the music started . . .

. . . only it wasn't the music she was expecting.

"WHAT IS THIS, CIRCUS MUSIC? I'm NOT a CLOWN!"

Wendy bellowed.

"Sorry, sorry—I don't know what happened . . ."

a voice behind the glass door said, and quickly replaced

the cheerful SILLY music with some **LOUD,**

BOLD marching music.

Wendy STOMPED purposefully into the room and

sat down in the dark velvet chair placed behind her slick-

looking desk. Walter had been told to wait until he was

called, and he didn't look very happy.

Wendy was still in silhouette and said, **"You can all**

clap now . . ."

There was polite applause, because no one really

wanted to be there.

"Good morning. How are we all doing?" Wendy

asked briskly.

Phillip Flop began to answer. **"We're all feeling—"**

Wendy held up her hand and stopped him. **"No**

need to reply, I'm not really interested. Although I

HOPE **it will be a good morning for ME. I'm on**

the wEDGE of my seat, WAITING to be impressed

today. My wonderful son, Walter, will be joining us for

the judging. You may ALL clap for Walter."

Walter STRODE in looking smug (although still

slightly pink from the paint). He sat down next to Wendy

and almost disappeared from sight.

"Someone get Walter a

cushion, or maybe two . . ." Wendy called out, and

glanced down at Walter. "Make that three cushions." The

cushions appeared quickly, and Walter stacked them on

his chair.

"Where were we . . . ?" Wendy asked now that the

problem was FIXED.

"As you all know, **THE GOLDEN SHOE AWARDS** are tomorrow and I intend to win. NOT for best special effects shoes or for the best shoe you can EAT. None of that nonsense, not this time. It's the top prize I want. NOW LET'S SEE WHICH OF YOU has made me the WINNING

WEDGES." She pointed to Betty. **"You first . . ."**

Betty Boot pushed her wedges toward Wendy and lifted up the glass dome to give her a closer look. Wendy tapped her nails on the desk. **"They look boring. What do they do?"** she asked, frowning.

"They make music, Ms. Wedge. Everyone needs music in their lives," Betty told her.

"Not everyone."
Wendy narrowed her
eyes as she watched

Betty take off her white coat and put the wedges on.

"Come on, Betty Boot, get on with it," Wendy

bellowed at her impatiently.

"Yes, hurry UP," Walter added.

Betty could feel Wendy's stony gaze on her. It was

making her fingers wobble. She tried to keep calm and

checked that the wedges were nice and tight on her feet.

Each one had lots of different-colored buttons, dials,

lights, switches, and lightning bolts, as well as TWO big

speakers on the front.

Betty took a moment to breathe, and then began to tap

one foot. The sound of tapping kept going after she stopped.

Then she clapped her hands and tapped her other foot. The

claps and taps were recorded and repeated to make a rhythm.

"Get on with it, will you?"

Wendy hissed.

Betty tapped her feet once more, and Wendy's VOICE started to come OUT of the shoe speakers.

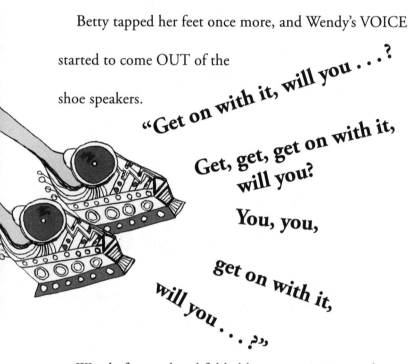

"Get on with it, will you . . . ?

Get, get, get on with it, will you?

You, you,

get on with it,

will you . . . ?"

Wendy frowned and folded her arms, waiting to be impressed.

"Then," said Betty, **"you can put it all together like THIS!"**

The wedges began to play music, with the lights flashing in time to the beat. Small wheels popped out from under the wedges, and Betty began to SPIN around in a circle.

She danced spectacularly, without any effort at all,

zooming forward, backward, and finishing with an

amazing super-speedy spin. Betty STOPPED and threw

her arms in the air. **"Ta-da! It's all in the WEDGES,**

no dancing skills required. You record the music and

the dance feature KICKS in, so anyone can DANCE in

these wedges."

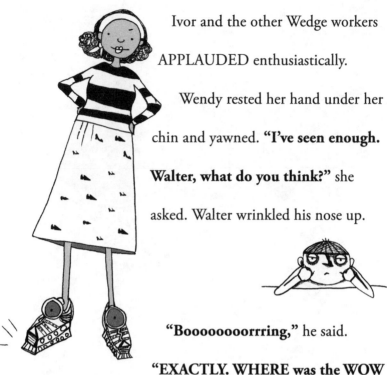

Ivor and the other Wedge workers
APPLAUDED enthusiastically.

Wendy rested her hand under her
chin and yawned. **"I've seen enough.
Walter, what do you think?"** she
asked. Walter wrinkled his nose up.

"Booooooooorrring," he said.

**"EXACTLY. WHERE was the WOW
factor, Betty? I've seen dancing shoes before. Do you
think all the shoemakers of Sneakerville or Shoecastle
will be quaking in their boots? I don't think so.**

"NEXT!" Wendy shouted.

Betty sat down again, slightly out of breath from the dancing.

"Well, I thought they were great," Ivor whispered.

"Thanks, but what was I thinking, making them FUN? For Wendy?" Betty whispered back.

Phillip Flop and Parminder Platform were up next. They both stepped forward.

Wendy rolled her eyes. **"Oh no, it's YOU two . . ."** Which didn't help their confidence.

"Ms. Wedge. In a world with many stresses and strains, we're all looking for something to CALM our nerves . . ."

"You're getting on MY nerves already. Hurry up . . ." Wendy snapped.

Phillip laughed nervously.

"Ms. Wedge, Parminder Platform and I will be demonstrating the magical, mind-healing POWER of WEDGE-I-TATION!" He gulped, then added, **"Like . . . meditation, but with wedges."**

"SERIOUSLY?" Wendy rolled her eyes some more. There was a box in front of them with gold fabric draped over it. Parminder stepped onto it with bare feet. She took a deep breath and closed her eyes.

"This had better be good," Walter murmured.

The thick gold fabric began to wrap itself around each foot, molding to Parminder's toes and coming together at each ankle. Parminder kept her eyes closed and her head up, HOPING it was all going according to plan.

"They don't look very . . . WEDGE-like," Wendy noted.

"Just wait," Phillip said. Parminder reached down and touched the fabric. It blew up like a balloon, forming itself into a WEDGE shape under her foot.

"Our wedges are temperature sensitive and can

 react to your mood and surroundings.

Imagine you're getting irritated because

you're stuck in a long line. They will

vibrate gently to soothe your worries

away," Parminder explained as the wedges began to pulse

all over, giving Parminder's feet a massage.

"**I NEVER wait. What else can they do?**" Wendy

snapped.

"They also turn any foot moisture into scented water that collects over the surface in tiny amounts. You can sit in the garden with your feet up, and beautiful birds and butterflies will be drawn to you."

"Allow us to demonstrate," Parminder said, and looked over to Phillip, who released a few butterflies and tiny birds. They fluttered in the air before coming to rest on Parminder's wedges. The birds tweeted and a feeling of sweetness and well-being washed over everyone.

"AWFUL! Who wants INSECTS

or BIRDS attacking their feet?

That wouldn't make me feel calm.

I'd be FURIOUS!

I've. Seen. ENOUGH!"

Wendy screeched. Her voice

made the birds and butterflies flee out the window.

"Now." She turned to Ivor, and a nasty smile curled

her mouth.

"YOU. IVOR FOOT. WHAT do you have for me?"

Ivor took a deep breath.

"The thing is, Ms. Wedge, Mr. Creeper said YOU already have my WEDGES?"

There was a silence while she watched him. Then Mr. Creeper took two slightly battered, damp camera wedges from his bag and dropped them on the table in front of Ivor.

"Oh! What happened?" Ivor asked, picking some wet leaves off the bashed-up shoes.

"What happened, Mr. Foot, is that Mr. Creeper kindly decided to TEST RUN them for you."

"He took my shoes?" asked Ivor.

"MY shoes, Mr. Foot. Remember, anything YOU make is mine. And while he was wearing MY shoes he managed to record something VERY interesting. Didn't you, Mr. Creeper?"

Mr. Creeper nodded as much as he could with his sore neck.

"Is there something you want to SHARE with me, Ivor? Anything at all?" Wendy asked in a VERY menacing voice. Before Ivor could say anything, Mr. Creeper turned on the camera wedges, and a faint, grainy image projected onto the wall. Everyone fell silent to listen, but the sound was scratchy. (That's putting it lightly.)

Sehoeibfoqeibfqbd cjnns bljb fly lnlspifjn djpwoj dpojepf pqpirbf fky.

"It really does get better," Mr. Creeper said.

"I hope so—for YOUR sake," Wendy told him. Ivor went quiet. This wasn't going well.

Mr. Creeper turned the camera wedge **OFF** . . .

and then **ON** as Wendy sighed loudly. This time, the

sound was crystal clear.

"Let me get this straight—you TOOK my flying

shoes from my workshop. THEN you used them to

FLY to the BRAND-NEW Wedge Town sign and paint

a heart over it?"

"It looks so much better now, Dad. You should see it."

"HOW did you even know

where to FIND the shoes?

I can't hide anything from

you two, can I?"

"Not really . . ."

Ivor cringed.

This was **BAD**.

"IVOR FOOT, you have been CAUGHT IN THE ACT!"

Wendy **FUMED**.

Mr. Creeper walked toward Ivor and held up a long TUBE in front of him, then slowly began pulling it apart to reveal . . .

. . . a piece of paper.

He rolled the paper out on the desk in front of him. It was so long it tumbled over the end and kept on going.

Wendy pointed at it.

"THIS is the contract that YOU signed and have broken. SEE? RIGHT here it states that any shoes you have made now or in the past ALL belong to Wendy Wedge. That's ME."

"I haven't broken my contract—the flying shoes were SALLY'S, not mine. SHE made them. You have ALL of MY shoes," Ivor tried to explain.

"Nice try, Ivor. But Sally isn't here, so why would I believe you? AND we have MORE evidence that you are a

TREACHEROUS LIAR."

186

She was definitely enjoying herself now.

"Ivor Foot, YOU are in possession of FLYING SHOES and OTHER FOOTWEAR that is ILLEGAL. You've broken WEDGE TOWN LAW not once, but TWICE," Wendy told him.

Chief Inspector Slingback nodded in agreement.

"That's right, Ms. Wedge, he has. Mr. Creeper has PROOF."

Ivor tried to stick up for himself.

"But I—"

"SHUT it, IVOR."

Wendy stomped her foot again, then gestured for Mr. Creeper to continue. He reached under his desk . . .

and very slowly brought out . . .

. . . a pair of fluffy white slippers.

Mr. Creeper placed them on the table and

patted their fluffiness.

Wendy slumped back dramatically,

because the mere SIGHT of slippers

made her feel faint with DISGUST.

"These . . . ILLEGAL THINGS

were found in your house, Ivor Foot. What have

you got to say ABOUT THAT?" Wendy demanded.

"They're not mine, Ms. Wedge. I've never seen them

before! SOMEONE must have put them there.

It's a slipper SETUP!"

Ivor tried to explain.

"Fluff and nonsense—

get them out of my sight!"

Wendy shrieked like they were the WORST things she'd

ever seen.

Officer Bunion began to read Ivor his rights.

"Ivor Foot, you are under arrest

for the possession of illegal

slippers AND for breaking

your contract with Wendy

Wedge by not handing over the FLYING shoes."

Wendy interrupted him. **"IF I don't get what I want,**

YOU'RE going to Shoe Prison for a very long time.

Take him away."

"WAIT! You CAN'T do this!" Ivor shouted.

"I can do ANYTHING I want, Ivor. I OWN this

town," Wendy corrected him.

"But the kids need me. I need them. They can't be left

alone! They've already lost their mother!" pleaded Ivor.

But Wendy just smiled. **"Well, I'm sure we can find**

a way around that. After all, they are little criminals

too. They dropped red paint on my Walter. Vandalized

the Wedge Town sign, which is public property. Both

criminal offenses."

"It was an accident! The flying shoes still need WORK—they went WONKY in the air. It wasn't their fault; the paint just spilled out," Ivor tried to explain.

"Did EVERYONE hear that? A room full of witnesses just heard you confess that your AWFUL children viciously ATTACKED my Walter!" Wendy shrieked triumphantly.

Walter stood up and added pompously, **"RUBY and BEAR need to be punished, Mom!"**

"You can't do this," Ivor shouted desperately.

"I can," Wendy told him.

"You can't," Ivor replied.

"I can too!" Wendy said, like a toddler having a tantrum.

Betty Boot could see the WHOLE situation was going very badly for Ivor and decided to do something about it while she still could. Quietly, she began to inch her way toward the door.

If she could slip out of Wendy's office before anyone spotted her, there was a chance she could find the Foot kids and keep them safe.

Luckily for Betty, Wendy's PIERCING voice was loud enough to cover up the sound of the door sliding open and shut.

"I CAN do what I WANT! HAND OVER THE FLYING SHOES OR YOU WILL NEVER WORK IN THIS TOWN OR ANY OTHER TOWN AGAIN. I COULD have you LOCKED UP FOR A VERY VERY VERY LONG TIME!" Wendy shouted.

"YEAH! SO THERE!" Walter added (even though there was really no need for him to).

"**Fine,**" Ivor said quietly. "**You win,**
Ms. Wedge. You can have the FLYING shoes.
BUT there's something you should know.
Those shoes aren't ready yet. They wobble
around in the air, and I'm the only person who can
fix them. So if you want to win THE GOLDEN
SHOE AWARD, you need to DROP these stupid
slipper charges." He took a deep breath. "**And leave**
Ruby and Bear out of this."

"**Just PUT them ALL in PRISON!**" Walter shouted
excitedly.

Wendy held up her hand for silence.

"**Oh, Ivor,**" she said coldly. "**Don't you**
realize I could get ANYONE in this room
to fix the shoes? Even Mr. Creeper
could do it."

Mr. Creeper whispered in Wendy's ear.

"What do you mean, you don't know how they work? What kind of an assistant ARE you?" Wendy asked, and Mr. Creeper shrugged. It was better to tell her now. Phillip Flop bravely stepped forward and spoke up.

"Ms. Wedge, Ivor's telling the truth. He IS the only person who could fix the shoes. None of us know how they work."

Chief Inspector Slingback cleared her throat. **"Also, Ms. Wedge, I just remembered—we might need a trial of some kind before putting anyone in prison."**

Wendy looked irritated. **"Really? Oh, how BORING."** She turned her back to Ivor. **"All right—hand the shoes over and then you get one chance to FIX them."**

"Yes, Ms. Wedge," Ivor assured her. "But first you have to promise to leave my kids out of all this."

"Don't make me lose my temper," Wendy muttered.

"Please, you have to promise." Ivor held out his little finger.

"What are you doing?" Wendy snapped.

"I'm asking you to make a pinkie promise," Ivor explained.

"This is ridiculous! Who on EARTH makes a pinkie promise?" She looked around the room. Officer T-Bar put up his hand.

"Sometimes I do."

"It does kind of work," Office Bunion agreed.

Parminder Platform and Terry Trainer both nodded as well.

195

Ivor took this opportunity to fill Wendy's thoughts with visions of flying. **"Ms. Wedge, picture it—you're flying effortlessly above everyone's heads. The judges are STUNNED by your genius. ALL the people in other shoe-making towns and cities who LAUGHED at your wooden flying shoes that never got off the ground have to watch as the judges award YOU THE GOLDEN SHOE AWARD."**

(Wendy's expression became dreamy and Ivor knew she was imagining flying triumphantly over an awestruck crowd.)

"Think of it. NO ONE will ever be able to laugh behind your back again," he continued.

"People laughed at me?" Wendy turned to Mr. Creeper. **"Is that true?"**

He didn't look her in the eye, but did a "maybe a little" sign with his hand—which was enough to set Wendy OFF again.

"HOW DARE they? I'll show those terrible tiny towns who's WHO."

"Exactly, Ms. Wedge. Think of the satisfaction you'll get from showing places like Shoehampton, Trainerville, Little Toehampton, **BIG Toehampton**, Shoecastle, Walking-on-Sea, and Bootchester . . . that YOU have the flying shoes they could only DREAM OF. They'll be AMAZED by YOUR fearless flying."

Ivor took a breath . . .

"Just remember: You have to leave Ruby and Bear alone. A pinkie promise HAS to be kept."

Wendy GLARED at him.

"Hmmmmmm . . ."

"Mom! Don't do it! It's a TRICK!" Walter shouted.

"It's not a trick, Walter. It's ASSURANCE that we'll both keep our ends of the bargain," Ivor said. He stretched out his little finger and wiggled it.

VERY reluctantly, Wendy stuck out her little finger.

"Pinkie . . . promise," she muttered, and snatched her hand back as fast as she could.

"NOW TELL ME WHERE the FLYING SHOES ARE!"

"Under the round table in my secret workshop. You'll need to press the tiles down in a special order to open it up—I'll write it down."

"I KNEW that table looked suspicious!"

Wendy snatched the code from Ivor and handed it to the SHOE POLICE.

"GO! And, Mr. Creeper, take him away!"

Wendy GLARED at Ivor.

"You can't!" Ivor shouted.

"Oh, I CAN—THIS is my insurance that YOU won't be leaving this building until I have the FLYING SHOES and THE GOLDEN SHOE AWARD in my hands."

Ivor tried to protest, but it was too late. With the dogs growling at his feet, Mr. Creeper led Ivor away.

Wendy turned to the others.

"What are you all LOOKING at? He's a SHOE CRIMINAL! No more TIPTOEING AROUND! Get back to work, all of you—or I'll arrest YOU TOO!" They all shuffled out of the room.

Chief Inspector Slingback took the code for the table, and the officers left to get the flying shoes. Ivor was escorted away by Mr. Creeper and the GROWLING DOGS. Wendy followed to remind Ivor that . . .

"No flying shoes means no GOLDEN SHOE AWARD—and NO escape for you, EVER!"**

"Mom! Don't forget you promised to punish the children!" Walter reminded her.

"Of course! I always keep my promises, Walter." Wendy smiled and THAT made Ivor MAD.

"Leave my kids OUT of this! You are a lia—"

Mr. Creeper shoved Ivor into a small room and locked the door.

"Left, Right—stay alert and on guard," Mr. Creeper ordered them.

NO!

grrrr

Wendy rubbed her hands together. Everything was going according to plan.

"I'll be WAITING for the flying shoes in my office, Mr. Creeper—DON'T LET ME DOWN," she said, glaring at him.

"WHAT Mom said,"

Hmmmm

Walter added, and STAMPED his foot down accidentally on Mr. Creeper's foot.

Mr. Creeper waited until Wendy and Walter were out of sight . . .

GENIUS

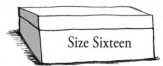

Size Sixteen

Betty Boot had BRAVELY made it out of Wendy's office. She dumped her white coat in the locker room. **"Stay calm,"** she told herself. She needed to get Ruby and Bear to safety. Wendy was out of **CONTROL!** Threatening to put everyone in PRISON was the last straw for Betty. She was going to find the kids and take them somewhere safe. Who knew what Wendy would do next? (Something TERRIBLE, that's for sure.)

Betty slipped out of the WOW building, walking fast. She had almost made it past the guards, when they STOPPED her. **"Ms. Boot?"** they said as their dogs growled at her feet.

"Yes?" she asked nervously.

"With **THE GOLDEN SHOE AWARDS** tomorrow, we're stepping up security. Please wear your ID next time, okay?"

"I'm sorry, I will. I was in a hurry."

Betty waved, and they waved back and lifted the barrier—which was a big relief.

It was a short walk to the school, where Betty could see the children were already playing outside for recess.

Good timing, she thought.

BUT getting inside the school without being seen was going to be tricky. UNTIL Betty spotted a loose panel in the wooden fence. **"Perfect,"** she whispered, and lifted it up. Betty squeezed herself in, then hid behind a large plant. She peered out through the leaves, looking for the kids. It wasn't long before her daughter, Chelsea, ran past. Betty made a loud **"Pssssssttttttt!"** noise to attract her attention.

Chelsea stopped. Was the plant talking? **"Pssst— Chelsea! It's me, Mom. Don't turn around."**

Chelsea turned around and stared at her mom in confusion.

"I'll explain EVERYTHING later. Right now I need you to go find Ruby and Bear and bring them back here, fast. Can you do that?"

Chelsea nodded yes.

"Are we leaving school early?" she asked hopefully.

"Yes. Go quickly and try NOT to bring any attention to yourself, okay?" Betty said, then motioned for her to GO.

"BEAR AND RUBY FOOT! WHERE ARE YOU? COME HERE QUICKLY!"

Chelsea's voiced BOOMED across the playground.

Betty shook her head. Chelsea kept shouting until she found them sitting on a bench. Unfortunately, Chloe Clog and Willie Winklepicker were there too, bothering them. Chelsea kept her distance and tried to get just Ruby's and Bear's attention . . .

. . . the best way she could.

"Oh, look! Our friend wants us to come over. Time to go," Ruby told Chloe and Willie.

But Willie and Chloe were both in a MOOD and wouldn't let them pass.

"What's the hurry?" Chloe said, LOOMING OVER Ruby.

"Can you move, please?" Bear asked nicely.

"Not until you show us your WEDGES. Walter told us to check to be sure you don't have any more illegal gadgets inside them," Willie snarled.

"YEAH—you two think you're SO SPECIAL when you're not," Chloe added.

"Show us your SHOES. NOW!" Willie demanded.

"They're the same as yours; leave us alone," Bear insisted.

"IF you have GADGETS hidden inside, we'll tell Walter, who'll tell his MOM, and you'll both get into a lot MORE trouble," Chloe sneered, and leaned really CLOSE to Ruby's face.

"Eeewwwwwww . . . There's something on your nose," Ruby said, frowning.

"Oh . . ." Chloe tried to check, then realized Ruby was joking. **"You're not funny,"** she snapped.

"You are, though!" Ruby laughed, and Chloe glared.

"Let me see your shoes! OR ELSE!" Willie said, STAMPING his foot down really hard.

"You've been hanging out with Walter Wedge for too long," Bear told him.

"HEY! Walter's my BEST friend!" Willie snapped back.

"And MINE," Chloe added.

"Walter's not a REAL friend—you'll see,"
Ruby told them.

"No, YOU'LL see," Chloe sneered.

"YEAH—you'll both be SORRY."
Willie grimaced, trying to be extra tough.

(This whole time, Chelsea was still FRANTICALLY trying to get

Ruby and Bear to come over.)

"See you later, Williegator!" Ruby said as she and

Bear pushed past.

"HEY—come back here!" Willie shouted.

"We should follow them . . ." Chloe said.

"Nah—let's find someone smaller to

annoy instead." Willie pointed to a girl

walking past (who smartly ignored them both).

"If Walter was here, she wouldn't

ignore us," Chloe sighed.

"No one would," Willie agreed. (It was true . . .)

Ruby and Bear finally joined Chelsea, who said:

"My mom told me to get you—it's urgent. Come quickly!"

They ran back to Betty (who was still hiding in the plant).

Relieved to see all three of the kids heading her way, Betty gave them each a hug and told them quickly, **"Your dad's okay, but we need to get you somewhere safe RIGHT NOW."**

"Away from Wendy Wedge?" Bear asked.

"YES—come on, follow me." Betty held up the broken fence panel so they could squeeze back through.

"Does this have something to do with the flying shoes?" Ruby whispered, trying to keep up with Betty.

"A little—but everything will be fine, I promise," Betty replied, sounding more hopeful than she felt.

They got away just in time. At the moment that they slipped under the fence, the shoe police arrived at the school gates with STRICT instructions to find those FOOT children.

It turned out that Foot was a popular last name in **Shoe Town**, and it took the shoe police a while to figure out that Ruby and Bear Foot had already left the building.

Betty knew some good shortcuts that got them back to the **Shoebox neighborhood** without being seen.

"We'll keep you out of Wendy's sight until it's dark," Betty told Ruby and Bear reassuringly.

Chelsea tugged on her mom's arm.

"Look who's there," she whispered.

It was Mr. Creeper.

"Quick, HIDE!" Betty said as they pressed up against the wall.

He headed into the Foots' house as two police cars pulled up outside Betty's house.

"There are shoe police EVERYWHERE. We can't stay here." Betty sighed.

"What do we do now?" asked Bear. This day was turning into a NIGHTMARE.

"We could hide in the burger place?" Chelsea suggested, her stomach rumbling.

"Not right now," Betty told her wearily.

Bear looked at Ruby. He could tell what was going through her mind.

"Don't even think about it."

"I wasn't going to sing—I was going to say, we should go to Bert's; he'll hide us," Ruby suggested.

"That's a GREAT idea! Good job, Ruby— let's go."

Betty took their hands, and they headed to Bert's shoe shop as fast as they could.

Size Seventeen

Betty looked around to make sure no one was following them, then opened the door to Bert's Brogues. A bell went PING, letting Bert know that he had visitors.

"Coming," he called out from his workshop at the back. Ruby pointed to the PROTEST SIGNS in the window.

"I made that one!" she said, smiling.

Betty admired Bert for fighting against World of Wedge taking over his shop. She knew he'd want to help them. Bert had been busy putting the finishing touches on an excellent pair of handmade brogues and was happy and surprised to see Betty, Chelsea, and the Foot kids all standing there.

"Hello, lovely people!" He grinned. **"What can I do for you? Are Wendy's 'wonderful' new school WOWs hurting your feet? Or has school just finished early today?"**

Betty wasted no time telling Bert all about Wendy Wedge getting her horrible hands on Ivor's flying shoes.

"**These two need a safe place to hide,**" Betty told him. "**And we're hoping you can help.**"

"**Of course! That Wendy Wedge is a real piece of work!**" Bert said bitterly. "**She's been trying to shut me down for ages. Mr. Creeper leaves her dogs outside my shop to scare my customers away. BUT I've been sneaking them sausages so they don't bother me anymore.**" Bert laughed. "**They're too FULL to move, and Mr. Creeper has no idea.**"

"**Good for you, Bert.**" Betty smiled.

"**That's so funny!**" Ruby said, and picked up a pair of handmade boots with a secret compartment in the heel.

"**Your shoes look really comfy,**" Chelsea told him.

"Well, Bert is a MASTER shoemaker. But right now we need to keep Ruby and Bear out of sight," Betty reminded everyone, and Bert ushered them into the workshop at the back of the store. It was nice to sit down after all the rushing around, and Betty needed some time to think.

"I want to be a master shoemaker one day," Ruby told everyone, looking around in awe.

"You'll need to be an apprentice for three years first, though Bert did it in two," Bear explained.

"How do you know that?" Bert asked, slightly surprised.

"You told me once and I'm good at remembering stuff," Bear said.

"He really is—it can be annoying," Ruby added.

"I'm not the only master shoemaker here. Betty, you've always made wonderful shoes."

"Wendy doesn't think so—she wasn't impressed with my music wedges!" Betty told him.

"What does SHE know?" Bert said furiously.

"She knows there's a chance of her winning **THE GOLDEN SHOE AWARD** tomorrow. IF Ivor can fix the flying shoes," said Betty.

"I hope he can figure it out FAST, for his sake," said Bert.

Bear and Ruby looked worried.

"Who's hungry?" Bert asked, to distract them.

"**ME!**" Ruby, Bear, and Chelsea put up their hands.

"We can't stay, Chelsea." Betty sighed.

"Pleeeeeease can I have some cake?" Chelsea pleaded.

"We really need to get back to the neighborhood to keep an eye on Ruby and Bert's home. We can let them know when the shoe police have left and the coast is clear," Betty explained. She hugged Ruby and Bear.

"Everything will be fine, I promise. We'll get you home when it's dark outside." Bert put some cake in a bag and gave it to Chelsea, which cheered her up.

"Thanks, Bert!" Betty smiled and hugged him too.

"What are old friends for? Us master shoemakers need to stick together."

Betty and Chelsea made their way back home— checking to be sure they weren't being followed.

Size Eighteen

SHOE Break
Be back
soon

Bert closed the shop and put a sign on the door. He hoped that would keep everyone away for a while. Ruby and Bear sat at the table as Bert put out some more food: bread and butter, cheese, a jar of lemon curd, sausages, olives, a sponge cake, and some sliced peaches in a bowl.

"Thanks for this, Bert," said Bear. "I hope Dad's okay."

"Me too. Stupid Wendy Wedge," Ruby replied, helping herself to some cake.

"I'm sure he's going to be fine. Sorry about the strange assortment of food!" Bert apologized.

"We don't mind," Bear said, eating some cheese while Ruby helped herself to a sausage.

"It's not fair—Wendy shouldn't win the award for Mom's flying shoes," Ruby said in between mouthfuls.

"I agree. In all my shoemaking years, I've never even gotten CLOSE to making a pair of flying shoes. I wouldn't know where to start," said Bert. "Your dad never told me they existed—he's good at keeping secrets. I wonder how Wendy found out?"

Ruby and Bear looked at each other. "It's all our fault," Ruby said miserably. "Dad kept them safe in his shoe workshop. But I woke up one night and saw him flying around the kitchen in them. Bear was asleep—snoring his head off."

"I wasn't snoring," Bear protested.

"You were too. Anyway," Ruby continued, "we borrowed the shoes to FLY up and paint over the new Wedge Town sign—I used the red paint you gave us, Bert!"

"YOU two did that?" Bert asked, surprised.

Ruby and Bear nodded enthusiastically.

"BUT the shoes wobbled in the air and GUESS who the paint spilled on?" Ruby asked.

"**Wendy?**" asked Bert with a shudder.

"**Almost—it was Walter. He kind of saw us flying away.**" Ruby sighed.

"**That's why Mr. Creeper is in our house now. He's looking for the shoes,**" Bear explained, then put a dollop of lemon curd on a peach slice.

lemon curd *peach slice*

"**Is that good?**" Ruby asked curiously.

"**I'll tell you in a second . . .**" He popped it in his mouth. "Mmmmm, sweet and delicious," Bear said.

"**Dad says the only thing Wendy Wedge cares about is her wedges and WINNING THE GOLDEN SHOE AWARD,**" Ruby told Bert.

"**Your dad's right. The humiliation of losing the last two awards hasn't helped. Everyone knew her WEIGHTLESS WONDER WEDGES were a disaster.**"

"**They were the lowest-scoring shoes ever in the history of the awards. And she lost the last THREE,**" Bear said, correcting Bert.

"That's made her more DESPERATE to win at any cost. I don't like the way Wendy is taking over EVERYTHING in this town. It's not right. Let's hope Mr. Creeper doesn't find the shoes," Bert said, getting even more furious. **"Your dad's secret workshop is FULL of stuff to hunt through. They *COULD* still be there."**

"Let's go back and check?" Bear suggested.

"We could enter THE GOLDEN SHOE AWARD with flying shoes, then!" Ruby was getting excited about this idea.

"I'm not sure that would work. We don't want to make things worse for your dad, do we?" Bert said.

"There MUST be something we can do?" Ruby asked, trying a slice of peach with lemon curd herself.

"What if Dad doesn't manage to fix the shoes? If Wendy doesn't win the award, I'm worried she won't let him go," said Ruby.*

"And even if she DOES, she'll probably keep him locked up making shoes for her forEVER," said Bear.

"We have to do something," said Ruby. "It's not fair for Wendy to win with Mom's shoes."

"You're right," said Bear, a glint in his eye. "It's time someone stopped Wendy. I think we should make a plan. But first, have some more bread."

Bear took a slice while Ruby tried an olive for the very first time.

(And the very last.)

*Foot note: She was right to be worried.

Ruby's anti-olive face.

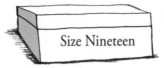

Size Nineteen

Night fell. Eventually the phone rang: It was Betty to say that the shoe police and Mr. Creeper had left the **Shoebox neighborhood**. Bert packed up the leftover sausages with some more cake for Ruby and Bear to take with them.

"Are you ready, kids?" he asked.

"We are SO ready," Bear said.

"Fingers crossed Mr. Creeper failed and the flying shoes are still there," Ruby added. They slipped out into the night and made it safely to their house. **"We'll need to be quick in case anyone comes back,"** Bert whispered.

Ruby and Bear followed him to the front door, which was already open.

Inside the house . . .

. . . it was a **MESS**.

There was stuff all over the place. Even worse, Sally's round table in the kitchen had been FORCED open and some of the beautifully painted tiles were cracked.

"I can fix them—don't worry," Bert reassured Ruby and Bear.

"That's Dad's workshop," Ruby told him.

"Very clever," Bert said, admiring the secret entrance.

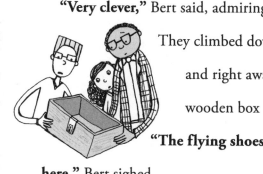 They climbed down the ladder and right away saw an empty wooden box on the floor. **"The flying shoes were probably in here."** Bert sighed.

"But we'll keep looking, just in case." Ruby had never seen inside the workshop before. It was full of fascinating objects. She crouched down to look at a low shelf and found a collection of interesting-looking books. She took one out that was tied up with a faded ribbon, and was about to read the title, when Bert said they should double-check upstairs.

Ruby slipped it under her sweater, and while Bear

and Bert searched through the rest of the house,

she took it back out and started to read. On

the cover in perfect handwriting, it said:

Sally Sandal's
Book of Shoe Designs
and Dreams.

"It's Mom's," Ruby whispered, then untied the

ribbon and opened the book. On every page of the

slightly yellow paper was a detailed drawing of some

very different types of shoes. Each design had tiny

handwritten instructions next to it.

"Wow . . ." Ruby was fascinated by it all.

She could hear Bear telling her to hurry up. Ruby closed the book, then squeezed it inside her bag before joining them.

Bert was standing in their bedroom and shaking his head. **"Oh my, Mr. Creeper and the shoe police really messed up your room too."** He sighed.

Bear laughed. **"No, this is what it always looks like in here. Ruby's just very messy. She has a LOT of stuff, especially overalls."**

"You're messier than I am, and I *like* overalls. I'm putting on my lucky pair right now," Ruby said.

"We could use all the help we can get," Bert said, then suddenly STOPPED talking, putting his hand up to his mouth.

"Shhh! Don't move a muscle," he whispered. They all FROZE. SOMETHING was making the porch boards creak outside.

Shoo leaped OUT

and scared them all.

"AGH!" Bert screamed.

"It's only Shoo," Ruby said. She picked the

cat up. "Calm down . . ."

"I'm trying." Bert sighed.

"I was talking to Shoo," Ruby said.

"We should bring Shoo with us to keep her safe," suggested Bear.

"Good idea," Bert agreed. "Now grab what you need and let's get to Betty's." Bert went to the kitchen window to check that the coast was still clear.

Ruby changed into her lucky overalls while Bear looked around one more time for the flying shoes. They were definitely gone.

"We'll have to go out the back door now—there's a lady talking to the shoe police officer outside," warned Bert.

"Is she holding a walking stick?" Bear asked.

"Yes."

"Mrs. Court," Ruby and Bear both said together.

"She is super nosy," Ruby explained.

"Hopefully she'll keep the officer busy," Bear added.

They snuck out the back door and made it to Betty's without anyone seeing them.

229

Chelsea wasted no time in helping Ruby and Bear feel at home. Betty had put a couple of sleeping bags in her room, which was a tight squeeze, but they didn't mind. No one had much space in the **Shoebox neighborhood**.

"Thanks for looking after them, Bert," Betty said, handing him some tea. **"No flying shoes, though?"**

"Gone. Mr. Creeper must have given them to Wendy by now," Bert said as he sipped his tea.

"I'm trying not to worry the kids, but it isn't easy," Betty whispered to Bert.

The full realization of what Wendy was up to was REALLY starting to sink in.

"If Wendy does use the flying shoes to win the award tomorrow, things will never be the same again," Bert said dramatically, shaking his head.

"What do you mean?" Ruby asked, interrupting their conversation as she and the other kids walked in.

"Nothing to worry about. After your dad gets home, she'll just BRAG about the award forever," Betty said, doing her best to play things down.

"And that's not all . . . Mark my words, no other town or city will EVER be allowed to make flying shoes. The World of Wedge will take over EVERY single shoe shop. We'll be forced to wear her big, clumpy wedges ALL the time just because SHE likes them. Wendy will use the flying shoes for WORLD SHOE domination. She already banned SLIPPERS. That's just a start. There'll be no room for shops like mine anymore. It's only a matter of time before she does SOMETHING SERIOUSLY sneaky to close me down."

Bert took a breath and stopped. He could tell from everyone's expressions he was getting a little worked up.

"OR, she might not win and everything will stay

the same, so don't listen to me,"

Bert said, trying to calm down.

(A little too late . . .)

"Why didn't you and Betty ever try making flying

shoes, Bert?" asked Ruby.

"I was wondering that too," Bear said.

"I did try," said Bert. "But I could

never get them to work.

It was too difficult. Your

mom, Sally, really was a genius! It must've taken her

years to get them right."

"That's true. Every shoemaker's DREAM was to invent the first pair of flying shoes," Betty added.

"Remember Wendy's Wooden Wonders? They never even got off the ground!" Bert laughed.

"And then there was her attempt at ROCKET shoes, which didn't work either," Betty reminded him.

weee

"They only stayed up for thirty-five seconds before they fell back down," Bear told them. He always knew good SHOE facts.

ARRRRGH!

"I really wanted to make shoes that could fly. I just never knew WHERE to start," said Betty.

"But what if you had something that SHOWED you EXACTLY how to make them? Could you do it then?" Ruby wondered.

"You mean like a manual?" asked Bert.

"It would have to be VERY detailed," said Betty. "But yes, probably."

"I'll be back in a second," Ruby told them, and went to get her bag.

"What's she up to?" Bear said suspiciously. Ruby came back with her bag and took out the BIG book.

"Where did you get that?" Bear asked.

"Dad's workshop," said Ruby. She carefully put the book on the table. "It's Mom's notebook. It's full of diagrams and notes."

They circled around to take a closer look.

"I recognize your mother's beautiful handwriting," Betty told them.

Bert looked closely at the detailed drawings. **"Oh my,
THIS is amazing. You're right, everything's HERE—all
the instructions are in this book. Your mom was SO
smart! This is perfect."**

Bert was very impressed.

"So could you make flying shoes NOW using Mom's instructions?" Bear asked.

Bert considered the diagram thoughtfully. "Maybe," he said. "It might be possible, with the help of another master shoemaker." He looked at Betty.

"Come on, Mom—make the flying shoes!" said Chelsea.

"You could ENTER **THE GOLDEN SHOE AWARD!**" Ruby said.

"RUBY, you're a genius!" Bear said.

"Finally, we agree on something!" Ruby exclaimed.

"Imagine the LOOK on Wendy's face." Bear laughed.

"It would be worth it just for that," Betty agreed.

"But do we have enough time?" Bert asked.

Betty suddenly stopped reading. "OH NO!" she said.

"What's wrong?" Bert asked.

"I can't help you, Bert. You'll have to make them by yourself," she said.

"Why?" he asked.

"Because I have exactly the SAME contract as Ivor. All the shoes I make belong to Wendy and WOW. If I even help you make the flying shoes, they'll belong to her."

"Is that legal?" Bert said.

"In Wedge Town it is. Wendy does what she wants."

"How will she know?" Ruby wondered.

"Trust me—she'll find out." The smile left Bert's face. Without Betty's help, making the flying shoes would be very difficult.

"You can do it, Bert," Ruby told him.

"Pleeeeeaasse, Bert! I really want to fly!" Chelsea asked sweetly.

"It's a lot of fun . . ." Bear said.

"It really is," Ruby agreed.

"You could SELL them in your shop. Flying shoes would be SO popular, Bert. You and Dad—together you'd make a FORTUNE!" Bear said.

"Wendy couldn't shut you down, then," Ruby added.

"They've got a point, Bert. What do you think?" Betty asked him.

"There's not much time. I'd HAVE to work ALL through the night to have a chance, and even then . . ." Bert said, thinking out loud. "But YES, I'll do it. It's about time we stood up to Wendy Wedge."

"GO, BERT!" Ruby and Bear shouted, and Chelsea cheered.

"Okay, I'd better get back to my workshop and get started. I just hope Ivor will be pleased about all this," Bert said.

"He'll be happy we're fighting back. This could change everything," Betty said.

"It's US against World of Wedge," Bear told them.

"It's SHOE WARS!" said Ruby proudly.

Betty carefully put Sally's book in a brown paper bag and gave it to Bert.

"I won't let you all down," Bert said, determined to do his best.

Wendy Wedge wasn't going to WIN this award with shoes that didn't belong to HER.

They all watched as Bert slipped out the back door into the night. Bert walked fast, clutching the precious book tightly under his arm and keeping his head down. He took a corner at full speed and bumped RIGHT

into . . .

Mr. Creeper.

The book slipped from under his arm and FELL to the ground.

"Look where you're going, will you?" Mr. Creeper

berated him. He was still sore from the wasp stings.

Bert hurried to pick the book up before Mr. Creeper

could see it.

"I'm so sorry, I wasn't paying attention," Bert told

him while trying to get the book back into the bag. His

fingers didn't seem to work, and he dropped

it AGAIN. Mr. Creeper

scowled—Bert

was holding him up.

"Sorry, it's way past my bedtime. I really must . . .

fly!" Bert managed to splutter. He clutched the book to

his chest and ran off down the road.

INSTANTLY, Bert wished he

hadn't said THAT word. **"Why did I**

say FLY?" he muttered to himself.

Mr. Creeper stood and watched him go.

Why is Bert in such a hurry? he wondered. Bert seemed nervous and jumpy. It got Mr. Creeper thinking that Bert might be up to something. This took his mind off his now very itchy foot. But not for long.

"When will this stop itching?"* he muttered.

*Foot note: Not for a long time.

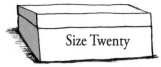

Size Twenty

Bert got away from Mr. Creeper as fast as he could. He hadn't seen the book, which was a relief. Bert needed to get busy shoemaking (the flying kind). Back inside the shop he quickly locked all the doors and pulled down the blinds. Then, safe in his workshop, he began to read all of Sally's instructions. They were clear, with helpful diagrams. To keep up his energy, Bert found himself strangely eating a sliced peach with some lemon curd on it*—and instantly regretted it.

"What was I thinking?" he asked himself before immediately eating another one.

It was going to be a very,

VERY long night.

Bert's sliced-peach-and-lemon-curd face

*Foot note: Don't try this at home.

Bert working super hard.

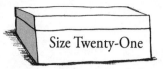

Size Twenty-One

Betty put the kids to bed and tucked them in, hoping they'd get some sleep.

"When will Wendy let Dad go?" Ruby asked her.

"Soon—he just needs to fix the wobble in the flying shoes," Betty replied. "I will go into WOW early tomorrow and make sure he's okay. I'm going to stand up to Wendy too."

Chelsea went to sleep, but Ruby and Bear lay awake for hours, thinking about everything that had happened.

"Bear, are you awake?" Ruby whispered.

"No."

"Yes, you are."

"Just kidding."

"What if Wendy doesn't let Dad go?" she said in a small, scared voice.

"She can't keep him there forever. It's against the law," Bear replied, which didn't make Ruby feel any better.

She got up and peeked through the window. She could see the big W building through the blinds. Ruby whispered, "Dad is in there somewhere, and . . ."

"And what . . . ?" Bear asked.

"And we need to do something. What if Wendy gets super mad and throws a FIT? She doesn't care about the law. I don't trust her. She might even HURT Dad. We've already lost Mom. We can't lose Dad too."

Bear sat up and looked at his sister bravely.

"You're right, Ruby, we need to get into WOW and rescue Dad. But how?"

"I can help you," Chelsea whispered. (She'd been awake and listening the whole time.) "I know where my mom keeps her badges."

245

"We don't want you to get in trouble," Bear said.

"If it was my mom locked up, I'd do the same," said Chelsea. "She was friends with your mom. She'd want to help."

"I miss Mom," said Bear quietly.

"Me too," said Ruby.

The kids lay there in silence for a moment. "Mom wouldn't take any nonsense from Wendy," Bear told them.

"Exactly—that's why we should do it. She wouldn't rest until Dad was rescued and back home," Ruby said.

Cat air punch

Shoo meowed like she agreed.

"I'll get the badges, but what about the dogs? They'll be wandering around," Chelsea reminded them.

"Oh yeah, those horrible dogs . . ." Ruby winced.

Bear and Ruby got dressed, and Chelsea handed them a badge for WOW, a backpack each, and a choice of masks. **"You don't want anyone to recognize you. There's a mouse or a unicorn,"** she explained.

"Good thinking. I call the mouse," Bear said.

"I wanted the mouse!" Ruby argued.

"Okay, you take it." Bear handed it over. **"It looks better on you anyway."**

"I've put in Bert's sausages too," said Chelsea. **"I'll put pillows in your sleeping bags so it looks like you're still here. My mom doesn't need to know you're gone— she'll just worry."**

"We're like secret agents," Ruby whispered excitedly.

"It's US against Wendy Wedge—let OPERATION SHOE WARS begin," said Bear, punching the air.

"If you say so." Ruby smiled.

With everything packed up, Chelsea let them out the back door. **"Good luck,"** she whispered, and waved goodbye.

Ruby and Bear's special bouncy school wedges made running faster. The **Shoebox neighborhood** was nice and quiet, and even Mrs. Court seemed to be asleep because her curtains weren't twitching like normal. But as they got closer to WOW, things got a LOT busier. There was a long line of vans and trucks waiting to go through the WOW gates. People were busy working all through the night to set up for **THE GOLDEN SHOE AWARDS**, and the guards were carefully checking EVERYONE coming in and out.

"Uh-oh," Ruby whispered.

"We might have to think of another way in," Bear said quietly. They kept watch from a safe distance while they thought about what to do next.

A van pulled up alongside them, and a man got out and opened the back door. It was STUFFED with balloons that almost flew out. He checked the address and said,

"This must be the place."

"Are you thinking what I'm thinking?" Ruby said to Bear.

"That depends. What are you thinking?"

"The door is still open—we can hide and get through the gates."

"That's what I was thinking too," Bear told her.

They hopped in the back with the balloons and tried

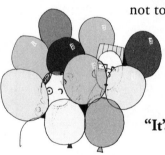 not to BURST any as the van drove up to the gates. The van stopped, and the driver began talking to the guards.

"It's **Larry Lace** delivering balloons for the awards. I should be on the list."

"Let's check . . . Oh, yes, here you are. You're very early."

"I'm trying to finish work and get home. It's my daughter's birthday tomorrow."

"Oh, nice. How old is she?" the guard asked.

"She's five. Little Tracy Lace."

"Hope she has a good one. Drive around to parking

bay three. Have a nice night," the guard said, and waved him through.

Bear and Ruby couldn't see each other through all of the balloons.

"As soon as the van stops, we slip out," Ruby whispered. She put her hand on the door to get in position.

"Take a bunch of balloons for cover," Bear suggested.

"Okay, let's go!" Ruby moved the balloons away from her face, then counted to three.

"One . . . two . . . three . . . go!"

They leaped out, dragging the huge bunch of balloons together and trying not to get tangled up.

Happy 5th Birthday, Tracy Lace!

"Hey, where are you going with those?"

It was Larry Lace.

Ruby and Bear froze.

"We're taking them to **THE GOLDEN SHOE AWARDS**, of course," said Bear.

Larry Lace squinted at them.

"**Wendy's orders,**" said Ruby.

"**Okay, then,**" said Larry Lace. "**Can you sign for them?**"

Ruby scribbled down *W Wedge* on the delivery slip and gave it back.

"**Thanks for the help. Have a good GOLDEN SHOE AWARDS. Who's going to win—any ideas?**" he asked.

"**We are,**" murmured Ruby.

"**Good for you,**" said Larry, not really listening.

He hopped back into his van and drove away.

"**That's what happens when you wear LUCKY overalls,**" Ruby said. She looked down and saw one of the guard dogs GROWLING at her feet.

"**Spoke too soon,**" she whispered.

"**Don't move. He wants a balloon,**" joked Bear.

"**He can have all of them,**" Ruby whispered.

"We need to get inside," Bear hissed.

"You keep him busy!" Ruby told him.

"How?"

"I don't know—talk to him?"

"Nice doggy . . ." Bear smiled as the dog growled.

"Aren't you cute?" But the dog growled LOUDER.

"Distract him with a balloon. I'll get the door,"
Ruby suggested, and got out her badge. She shuffled
toward the door and waved the badge over the scanner.

BEEP!

BEEP!

The door CLICKED open just in time.

Grrrrrrrrr.

"GO! QUICKLY!" Ruby shouted at Bear.

"What about the balloons?"

"LEAVE them!"

So he did, sending the little dog into a furious frenzy
as the doors closed behind them and ALL the light
disappeared.

They were in

complete darkness.

"Where are you?" Ruby asked.

"Here," Bear told her.

"Where?"

"HERE."

They could feel the

hallway walls, but

it was very hard to

see where they

were going.

"At least no one can see us.

That's a good thing,"

Bear whispered.

"I think I know

which way to go.

Follow me,"

Ruby told him, and

started to walk . . .

PING!

ALL THE LIGHTS

WENT ON AND

DAZED THEM.

"Movement sensors. Not ideal," Bear said, blinking

in the BRIGHTNESS.

"At least we can SEE now," Ruby told him.

"Look up there," Bear said, pointing at the ceiling.

"Cameras. Masks on before someone recognizes us."

Ruby and Bear made a run for it, activating the

movement sensors as they went. At the end of the hall

there was another door. Gasping for breath, they took out

the badges.

They went through slowly and looked carefully around the corner.

Grrrrr! Wooof! WOOOF! WOOOF!

"More dogs! Do you think they're looking for us?" Ruby whispered.

"I don't want to find out. Let's head over there." Bear pointed to another door. They pressed themselves up against the walls and slid along slowly, using their badges again.

BEEP! They were in.

"These badges are VERY useful. Thank you, Chelsea," Ruby said. So far, everything was going according to plan . . .*

*Foot note: But not for long.

They were inside a big room. There was a large
W-shaped desk and the walls were covered with pictures
of Wendy, staring down at them fiercely.

"This must be Wendy's office," Bear whispered.

"How can you tell?" Ruby asked.

"Because of . . ."

"I'm joking. Now, where would Wendy keep Dad?"
Ruby asked, looking at the three doors in front of them.

As they were deciding which way to go, a VERY
familiar shadow walked past the frosted glass on the right
side of the room. The sight of Wendy
Wedge helped
to make up
their minds
FAST!

"That's Wendy!
Quick! Let's get out of here!"
Thump
Thump
Thump

They slipped out of Wendy's office and found themselves in the main part of the World of Wedge building. The workshops were all full of white-coated

people looking serious as they finished their WEDGES for **THE GOLDEN SHOE AWARDS**. Ruby and Bear tiptoed past each window. They popped their heads up and down like meerkats, looking out for their dad.

"Why are they still working on those wedges? Wendy has Dad working on the flying shoes," Ruby said.

"Because she's greedy and wants ALL the prizes," Bear whispered, then pointed to a worktable. **"Look! There's Dad's camera wedges."**

"We could use them NOW to help look for Dad with the camera," Ruby told Bear. They didn't have to wait long before the door opened and the white-coated shoemakers began to leave.

Bear and Ruby kept quiet and hid behind the door. Then they slipped into the workshop as the door closed behind them. **"HERE—you wear one wedge and I'll wear the other so we'll BOTH have a camera,"** Ruby suggested. She took a control panel and put it on her wrist, then passed the other one to Bear.

"Ready—let's test them. Camera up," Ruby said into her control panel, and made the camera FOCUS on Bear.

"Whhooooaaa, I can see you! Wave . . ." she told him.

"Ruby, we don't have time," Bear whispered.

"There's ALWAYS time to annoy you. I'm just testing how they work, that's all."

"**Good point, let's go,**" Bear said.

"**Where do we start? This building is HUGE,**" Ruby asked.

"**I don't know, but we better hurry,**" Bear told her.

"**We've got to find Dad. He MUST be here somewhere.**"

They set off down the hall again.

(Dad was closer than they knew . . .)

Size Twenty-Two

WOOooooFff
WOOOofffff
Woooooffff
Wooffff

Ivor could hear talking outside

the room he was locked in.

He began rattling the door

handle as hard as he could and

yelling, **"HEY! Let
me out!"**

But his shouting only made

the dogs standing guard—Left and Right—BARK

LOUDLY.

Ivor's fear was now OFF

the charts. Were the kids okay?

How long was Wendy going to keep

him for? And WHO had his flying shoes?

They still needed adjusting to get rid of the

WOBBLES. He'd told Wendy he'd FIX them in time for

THE GOLDEN SHOE AWARDS.

But so far, no one had brought them back.

Maybe they didn't believe him? Ivor always kept his promises, unlike Wendy Wedge, who just kept making up random laws to benefit herself. Wendy could still CHARGE Ivor with owning the slippers and put him in PRISON.

What was so wrong with slippers anyway?

"I wish I had those flying shoes right now. I'd ESCAPE—FLY out that door over everyone's heads," Ivor muttered. He was starting to get tired.

"How am I EVER going to get out of here now?" he said to himself.

Ivor was in an impossible situation.*

*Foot note: Or so he thought.

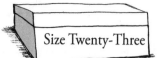

Size Twenty-Three

"**W**e look like SUPERHEROES!" Ruby

pointed at the impressively large shadows

they were casting in front of them.

"**Don't stop—someone might see us,**" Bear

told her—just a little too late. Mr. Creeper

and Chief Inspector Slingback were

WALKING STRAIGHT toward them.

"**Do you mean someone like . . . them?**"

Ruby said. "**Quick, HIDE!**" In a panic, they both ran in

different directions.

Bear saw a door and used his badge to get in quickly.

"**That was close!**" he said, expecting to see Ruby following

him. She wasn't there—though something else was . . .

Gggggrrrrrrrrrrrrrrrr . . .
GGGrrrrrrrrrrrrrrrrr . . .

Guard dogs.

"Uh-oh . . ."

Bear backed up as Left and Right moved closer. He bumped into a locker, fumbled for the door, then jumped inside, slamming it SHUT just in time. The dogs ran at him and were BARKING nonstop. Things couldn't get any worse, could they? (Yes, they could.) Mr. Creeper and Chief Inspector Slingback walked in.

"Pipe down, you two! It's only US," Mr. Creeper said as he walked past the locker. **"The code Ivor gave us for the weird table worked, but the flying shoes were GONE. We looked everywhere in that house,"** Bear heard Mr. Creeper say.

"Ivor Foot knows more than he's telling us. It's time to get TOUGH," said Chief Inspector Slingback.

GRRRRRRRrrrrrrrrrrrrr

Bear kept watching from inside the locker as they

waved their badges over another door and

pushed it open. For a split second, Bear

caught sight of . . .

DAD!

HE WAS IN THAT ROOM!

YES! I FOUND him!

he thought.

Bear was SO relieved—until he

remembered the dogs.

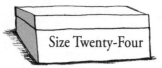

Size Twenty-Four

Chief Inspector Slingback was having a moment.

"YOU LIED TO US, IVOR FOOT! THE FLYING SHOES WEREN'T there! WHAT HAVE YOU DONE WITH THEM, IVOR? WE NEED to FIND them NOW or Wendy will be unbearable!"

"You mean MORE unbearable," Ivor corrected him.

"Think of your CHILDREN, Ivor. No **GOLDEN SHOE AWARD** means not seeing your kids for a VERY **LONG** time,"

Mr. Creeper reminded him.

"Are you SURE you went to the right house?" Ivor asked.

"YES! OF COURSE WE DID!"

roared the chief inspector, then paused

and turned to Mr. Creeper. **"We did—didn't we?"**

"I think so . . ." Wendy's assistant said.

"Are you POSITIVE?" Ivor said.

"YES! Stop making it OUR fault! WHERE are they, Ivor?" Chief Inspector Slingback was getting angrier.

"In the secret room, where I left them," Ivor insisted.

"WELL, they're not THERE now. If Wendy doesn't get those shoes by the morning, YOU have a VERY BIG WEDGE-SHAPED problem."

"Maybe your KIDS took the SHOES!" Mr. Creeper suggested.

"Why would they do that?" Ivor asked.

"YOU tell us!" Mr. Creeper started to scratch all over his body.

"It's not the first time they've been in trouble, IS it?" Chief Inspector Slingback said.

"The shoe police told us they weren't in school. They've gone missing with the shoes," Mr. Creeper told Ivor.

"That's ridiculous! They've been sick: totally covered in SPOTS. Ask Wendy; she saw them."

Both Chief Inspector Slingback and Mr. Creeper looked puzzled.

"They are VERY infectious. You don't want to go NEAR them." Ivor was saying anything he could to keep them away from Ruby and Bear.

"Nice try, Ivor. It's only a matter of time before we FIND them. And you'd better HOPE they do have those flying shoes," Mr. Creeper told him.

"What kind of people are you, picking on small children? **Shoe Town** used to be a great place to live until Wendy Wedge took over. You can't trust her; she's always breaking her promises. I BET she's already broken some promises to you."

Mr. Creeper and Chief Inspector Slingback looked quickly at each other. (Ivor could tell he was right.)

"We'll be back," they said in slightly sinister voices, and left Ivor in a HUFF.

Left and Right were STILL sitting in front of the locker where Bear was hiding.

"What are you doing THERE? You should be guarding Ivor," Mr. Creeper told the dogs, and pointed to the PLACE where he wanted them to be.

They scurried over and slid down to the ground.

Bear held his breath until he heard the door shut behind Mr. Creeper and Chief Inspector Slingback.

DAD was SO close!

Bear just wanted to SEE him and let him know that he and Ruby had come to RESCUE him.

But how was he going to get past the dogs?

"SAUSAGES!" whispered Bear.

He had them in his bag.

It was worth a try.

Bear took out the leftover sausages wrapped in foil, and right away, the dogs began to growl and SNIFF the air. He opened the locker door just enough to poke out the camera and check **exactly** where the dogs were. It didn't take long to find them. The dogs could SMELL the sausages. They were getting closer and hungrier.

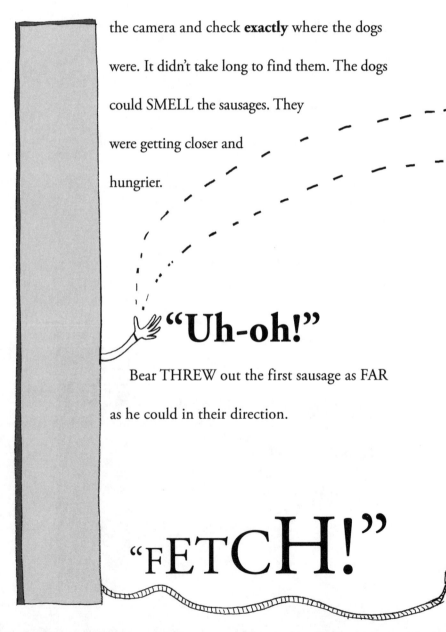

"Uh-oh!"

Bear THREW out the first sausage as FAR as he could in their direction.

"FETCH!"

The sausage gracefully F L E W through the air,

then—**SNAP!**—Right jumped up and CAUGHT

it in his mouth. Next, Bear aimed for LEFT—who, not

wanting to miss out, HURLED himself at the sausage.

SNAP!

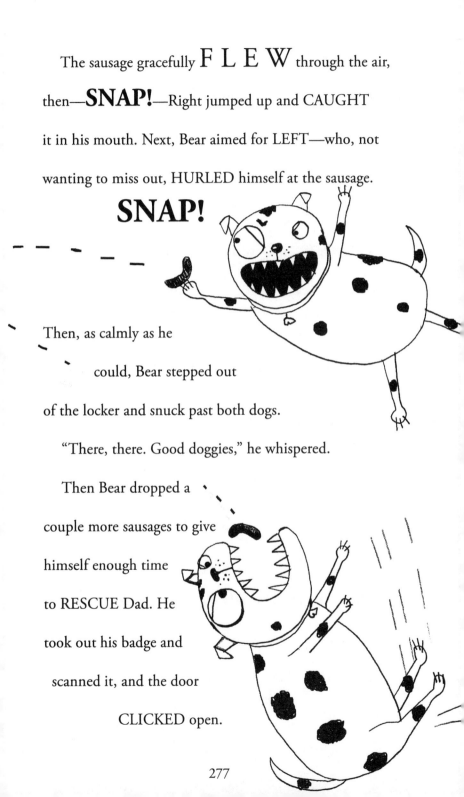

Then, as calmly as he

could, Bear stepped out

of the locker and snuck past both dogs.

"There, there. Good doggies," he whispered.

Then Bear dropped a

couple more sausages to give

himself enough time

to RESCUE Dad. He

took out his badge and

scanned it, and the door

CLICKED open.

277

"DAD!" Bear called out.

"Bear? What are you doing here?" Ivor said in surprise.

"We came to rescue you!" Bear told him, and they hugged each other tightly.

"WE?" Dad repeated.

"Ruby's here too—we got separated running away from Mr. Creeper and the shoe police."

"WHAT? Where is she?" Dad was trying to take it all in.

"She ran back toward where we came in. Let's go—I don't have many sausages left," Bear said, which just made Dad even more confused.

"Okay—but what about the dogs?" he asked.

Bear opened the door to reveal the dogs still munching on their sausages.

"They're happy. I've only got one piece left to get us out, though," Bear said.

"Come on—what are we waiting for?" Dad smiled at Bear.

"Which way did Ruby go?"

"In the direction of Wendy's office, I think," Bear said.

"Follow me." Dad checked to be sure there was no one around before they hurried to find Ruby.

"I NEVER know what you two are going to do next," Dad said to Bear as they ran.

"I do—we're going to win **THE GOLDEN SHOE AWARDS,**" Bear told him.

Ivor wasn't really taking anything in. He was trying not to think about what would happen if they ALL got caught.

"I hope Ruby's okay," he said as they ran down the hallway.

"Don't worry—Ruby's good at squeezing into small spaces. She'll find somewhere safe to hide,"* Bear reminded Dad.

 *Foot note: Maybe, maybe not.

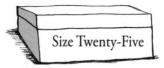

Size Twenty-Five

Hiding behind Wendy's enormous desk probably wasn't the best place Ruby could have chosen. She'd *R U N* as fast as she could away from Mr. Creeper and Chief Inspector Slingback and found herself right BACK where she'd started—in Wendy's office.

But if she was QUICK, she might find a CLUE to where Dad was being kept.

I'm going to investigate, she thought, and crept out to look around. Everywhere she walked, the EYES of Wendy's paintings seemed to follow her—which was creepy. Ruby shivered and made a face, then picked up a photo of Walter as a baby and laughed.

"Ha! He's always been a dork,"

she whispered.

"And there's Mommy dork," Ruby joked, looking at a picture of Wendy. She was wearing some zigzag-patterned wedges and, WEIRDLY for Wendy, she was smiling. **"Chilling,"** Ruby muttered, and kept

moving until she came to another door. Curiosity got the best of her, and she couldn't resist snooping in there too. She opened the door.

"THIS must be where Wendy lives. It's SO much bigger than our Shoebox house. Bear has to see this."

Ruby whispered into her wrist control, **"Turn camera on."**

Her wedge opened up, and the arm stretched out, recording the HUGE front room with the W-shaped sofa, chairs, and anything else she thought looked interesting.

Next, she stepped into Wendy's bedroom. There was

the BIGGEST four-poster bed Ruby had EVER seen.

(It was the only four-poster bed she had ever seen.)

Ruby resisted the URGE to JUMP on it, but only

because she noticed a WIG. She put it on and filmed

herself looking fierce. **"Can you believe Wendy wears**

a wig?" Ruby whispered to the camera. **"And check**

out the SIZE of this shoe closet." Ruby took off the

wig and pushed back the curtains to reveal Wendy's

collection.

"Whoa—how many pairs of wedges do you need?"*

Ruby whispered.

*Footnote: Turns out, a lot.

Inside there were rows and rows of different types of wedges, none of which looked comfortable: metal wedges with nuts and bolts holding them together, modern angular wedges, and lots of variations of Wendy's fierce-creature wedges.

Ruby couldn't resist trying a pair on. She slipped her foot inside a metal wedge and balanced on one leg, putting her hand on the wall to steady herself. *How can Wendy walk in these?* Ruby thought as she WOBBLED and lost her balance. She put her hand out as she fell and pushed a picture right into the wall.

"**Uh-oh . . .**"

Ruby watched as a WHOLE different cupboard suddenly sprang open. It was a secret shoe cabinet. THESE wedges looked very different from the ones in the show. They looked softer, with more colors and patterns. Some had feathers and scales and all kinds of textures too.

She picked up a pair and TOUCHED the shapes on the side. They instantly changed color.

"Wow."

There was another pair that had an interesting zigzag pattern. **"Crazy,"** she whispered. Something told her this was a good thing to record. But as the camera took in all the WEDGES, Ruby suddenly froze. She could hear FOOTSTEPS. Heavy, thumping footsteps. The kind of footsteps that could only come from one person. **"Uh-oh . . ."**

It wasn't hard to guess WHO was about to come in.

(Take another guess . . .)

Thump

Thump

Thump

It WAS Wendy Wedge.

Ruby ran into the bedroom and threw herself UNDER the four-poster bed, seconds before the door SWUNG open and in marched Wendy.

Ruby could see and FEEL the HEAVY creature wedges THUMP past her.

"I'm surrounded by idiots. Just FIND the flying shoes. How hard is THAT?" Wendy was talking to herself.

She began to take off her ENORMOUS shoulder pads and put them on the stand.

The creature wedges were SO close to the edge of the bed, their sensors were picking up on Ruby and GROWLING. Ruby couldn't move a muscle.

"If Ivor Foot hadn't been so SELFISH and just handed over the flying shoes in the first place, I wouldn't be in this position! Oh! My FEET are killing me."

Wendy walked past again and SAT on the bed. Ruby grimaced.

"My aching toes," Wendy cried again. "It's time for extreme measures."

Wendy got up to look for something and disappeared into her shoe closet. THIS was Ruby's chance to make a run for it. There wasn't much time. But as soon as she began to roll out from under the bed . . .

. . . Wendy came back, BAREFOOT.

Ruby was forced to fling herself back under the bed—FAST. Wendy walked up and down and then STOPPED. Her bony feet were SO close to Ruby's face. Ruby held her breath (for lots of reasons). Wendy's feet looked like they'd spent YEARS being squeezed into very uncomfortable wedges. (Because they had.)

Ruby closed her eyes and held her breath. It was all too much.

She tucked herself as FAR back as she possibly could.

"After the DAY I've had, I need to put my FEET up and get some rest. Tomorrow's GOLDEN SHOE AWARD is going to be VERY special for me. Maybe I'll just read a few pages of my book before bed."

PHUFF

PHUFFF

Two things landed in front of Ruby.

She opened her eyes to see Wendy's gnarly old feet sliding right into . . .

A PAIR OF SLIPPERS
FLUFFY PINK SLIPPERS.
With POM-POMS.

Ruby put her hand over her mouth to

STOP herself from GASPING!

Wendy was wearing slippers. Fluffy, cozy, illegal slippers. No one would EVER believe it: The owner of World of Wedge, the MOST powerful shoemaking company in town, was in front of her right now wearing soft, comfy SLIPPERS.

Wendy sat down in a chair and got out her book. She put her slippered feet on a comfy stool and began to read. Ruby stayed perfectly still.

It was clear Ruby was going to be STUCK hiding for a while. She'd have to wait for Wendy to go to bed and fall FAST asleep before trying to escape again.

And that could take a VERY long time.

RA**SSS**ssss**PPₚPPPPP**P!

RAAA**SSS**ssss**PPPP**P!

But it didn't.

Wendy's crooked mouth

dropped open and a loud

SNOORRRrrrrrrrreee came

out immediately.

THIS time Ruby

took a chance to

LEAVE and get to safety.

She rolled out from under the bed and began to TIPTOE

across the room. She took a small step forward . . .

CrEak!

Ruby winced.

Her second step was quieter.

Third step,

fourth step . . .

She was almost out.

But THEN . . .

KNOCK

    KNOCK

      KNOCK

Ruby FROZE like she was playing freeze tag.

She turned to glance at Wendy, whose eyelids were

beginning to FLICKER. She was WAKING UP!

Ruby quickly ran behind Wendy's chair and crouched

down.

"Huh? WHO'S THERE?"

Wendy mumbled, and stood up.

"DON'T come in!" she hollered. **"I'll be there in a second."** She got up, and shuffled to the closet in her slippers.

"WHAT now? No peace for ME," Wendy grumbled.

KNOCK! KNOCK! KNOCK!

"I said, WAIT!" Wendy shouted. She put on

her shoulder pads and went to the door.

Ruby listened carefully.

"Ms. Wedge, I'm so sorry to disturb you . . ."

"YOU should be. This BETTER be IMPORTANT!" she yelled.

Ruby couldn't see who Wendy was yelling at.

"WHY DIDN'T YOU COME AND

TELL ME EARLIER? Idiots!"

Then the door closed and Ruby could hear the sound

of Wendy

STOMP
STOMP
STOMPING away.

It was NOW or never.

Ruby peeked out from behind the chair, then RAN for

the door, fumbled in her bag for the BADGE, clicked the

lock open, and went through . . .

"Uh-oh . . ." Ruby whispered as the door closed

behind her.

This didn't look right at all.

What was this place? It didn't feel like an office or part of Wendy's apartment. It was . . . darker. Ruby could just about make out the rows of large glass tanks.

"What are these?" Ruby wondered as she edged closer to the nearest tank. The bugs inside began to flicker with tiny lights. "That's SO cool!"

She watched the mini light show, then moved on to another tank. "I'd better film THIS," Ruby whispered to herself.

Dozens of beetles were scuttling around, their shiny gold wings flickering. Ruby went from tank to tank watching the weird, exotic-looking bugs and creatures.

"Is this some kind of zoo?" she wondered. She touched the side of a tank and the wings of the bugs rippled and pulsed with different colors.

"That's amazing," said Ruby. She did it again. The rippling movement reminded her of something, but what?

She peeked into more tanks and saw bright red shiny bugs and HUGE butterflies with dazzling patterns on their wings. There was a larger cage full of tiny birds— their wings were covered with gorgeous jewel-colored feathers.

Ruby had never seen anything like this before. There were even more tanks HIGHER up that she couldn't see into. **"I wish I was taller,"** she murmured, then noticed a small set of wooden steps. **"Just what I need."**

Ruby pulled the steps closer and climbed up to the top layer of tanks.

She still couldn't see anything. **"Maybe they're empty. I'll check."**

Ruby spoke into her wrist control: **"Camera UP."** It weaved from side to side, searching for something to film. **"Camera—tap the glass,"** she whispered.

Tap

   Tap

      Tap

         Tap.

Still nothing. Ruby took one step back down the ladder, when something moved . . .

... The WHOLE tank **HISSED.**
It was full of SNAKES!
SCARY, **POISONOUS,**
ZIGZAG-PATTERNED
SNAKES!
Ruby YELPED and stumbled
back down the ladder.

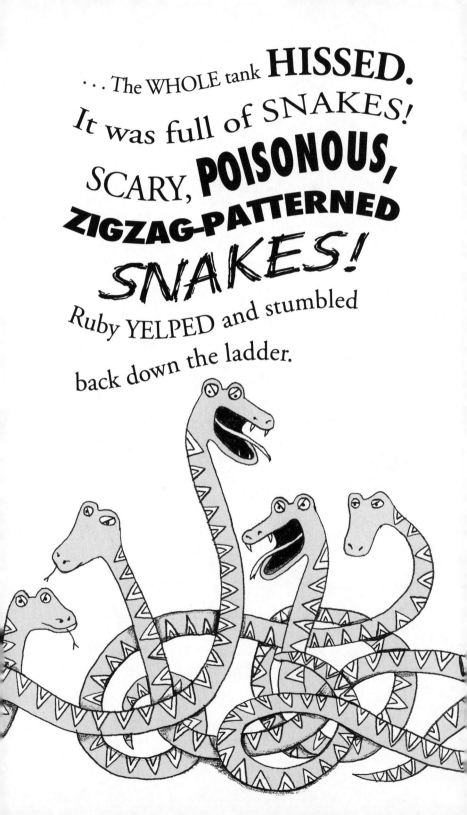

There were SO many SNAKES. What were they doing here? This whole place was freaky, and Ruby didn't like it at all.

But there was something about the snakes that looked weirdly familiar. Ruby cautiously climbed back up the ladder for another quick look.

"Where have I seen these before?" she said. She filmed them slithering around, looking angry at being disturbed.

Ruby knew she had to get out of there. She climbed back down, and this time she found the right door

and RAN as fast as

she could . . .

. . . RIGHT into Dad!

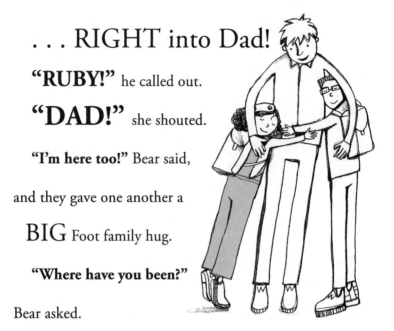

"RUBY!" he called out.

"DAD!" she shouted.

"I'm here too!" Bear said,

and they gave one another a

BIG Foot family hug.

"Where have you been?"

Bear asked.

**"You are NOT going to

believe what I just SAW!"**

Ruby said. Dad looked down at her feet.

"You're wearing the other camera shoe!"

**"I've been filming, Dad. I can't wait to show you!

It's going to change everything."**

**"How did you even get in? Actually, don't answer

that now—we'd better get out of here."** Ivor knew

they didn't have much time.

"Where did you hide, Ruby?" Bear asked as they followed Dad.

"Lots of places—behind Wendy's desk, under her bed, behind her chair . . . I saw a LOT of scary things."

"I'm not sure I want to know . . ." Dad said. He still couldn't believe his kids had come to his rescue. They were as brave and as brilliant as their mom—she would have been so proud of them.

Ruby and Bear followed Dad out of the WOW building and back to Betty's house as quickly as they could. Dad knew his ESCAPE would make Wendy even more **FURIOUS**. She'd go **MAD** with **RAGE**. He could imagine her face.

Ivor smiled. His kids were the best.

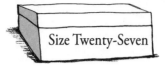

Size Twenty-Seven

The sun was coming up when Chelsea knocked on her mom's bedroom door, holding a cup of tea.

"Thank you, Chelsea—that's nice of you. What have you broken?" Betty asked, only half joking.

"Nothing." Chelsea smiled. "Someone's here. I thought I'd come and tell you."

"WHO? Not Wendy Wedge!" Betty put down her cup of tea.

"No—you would have heard HER coming from a MILE away. It's a surprise!"

The last person Betty was expecting to see was Ivor. "Are you okay? How on earth did you escape Wendy's clutches?"

Betty asked.

"It's all thanks to these SUPERHERO children. They got me out," Ivor told Betty, who was stunned.

"Don't worry, Mom—it's all fine. We put your WOW badges back," Chelsea explained.

"You used my badges?!" Betty asked. "What about the security cameras?"

"We had masks and balloons," Ruby explained.

"Don't worry about it now, Betty. We need to figure out WHAT to do next. Wendy's not going to stop looking for us," Ivor told her.

"You're right—the shoe police will be out in full force. In case anyone forgot, it's **THE GOLDEN SHOE AWARDS** today. And I have to go to work and pretend that EVERYTHING'S fine. Which isn't going to be easy," Betty said.

"At least Mr. Creeper didn't find the flying shoes. That's something. Speaking of which, where can they be?" Ivor said. "I wonder whether they're still in the house."

"No," said Ruby and Bear, answering at the same time.

"SO, let me get this straight. Wendy doesn't have the flying shoes. Mr. Creeper doesn't have them, and they're NOT at our house. WHO has them, then?"

Ivor put his head in his hands.

"Well, BERT is trying to make a new pair," Betty said, which didn't make any sense to Ivor at all.

"He's using the special book of Mom's that I found. Bert's going to make the flying shoes and WIN **THE GOLDEN SHOE AWARD** for YOU and MOM," Ruby told Dad happily.

"Bert's the only shoemaker who hasn't signed Wendy's terrible contract. He's been up all night working on them," Betty tried to explain to Ivor, whose head was spinning now.

"But if we can't find the flying shoes, Wendy will put me in prison. For owning slippers. Which weren't even mine!"

Ruby JUMPED up.

"That's it! Slippers! I knew there was something I wanted to tell you!"

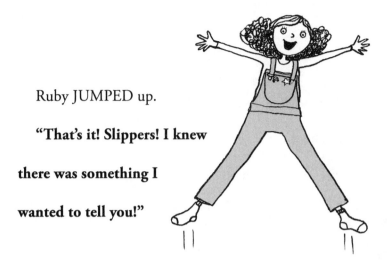

"What is it?" Dad asked,

when suddenly there was a knock on the door.

"Who's that?" Betty asked suspiciously, and peeked

out the window to see three shoe officers standing there.

"You all go and HIDE. We'll deal with it, won't we, Chelsea?" said Betty.

"Leave it to me, Mom . . . I've got this," said

Chelsea, and she went to answer the door.

Size Twenty-Eight

There were three police officers

outside and one (hungry-looking) small dog.

"**Is your mom here?**" Officer Sneaker asked

Chelsea. She gave the officers a sweet smile.

"Yes," said Chelsea. "**Do you want to talk to her?**"

"**Yes. We need to come in and search your house,**"

Officer Scarpin said.

"**Are you allowed to do that?**" Chelsea asked.

"**Yes,**" Officer Trainer told her, frowning.

"**Who says?**"

"**Uuuuumm, Wendy Wedge, that's WHO.**"

"**But what if I don't want to let you in?**"

The police were confused.

"**You have to,**" Officer Trainer told her.

"**No, I don't—what's the password?**"

Chelsea asked.

"**This isn't a game,**" said Officer Scarpin.

"**Password, please, and I'll let you in.**"

The officers talked among themselves and then

turned back.

"**Okay—is it SHOES . . . ?**"

"**Nope. Try again.**"

"**WEDGES?**"

"**NO!**"

"**LOOK, kid, we don't**

have all day. Just let us in."

"**You have to say the password,**" Chelsea said firmly.

She was really, really enjoying herself.

"We're coming in, ready or not," Officer Trainer said.

"The password's PLEASE. You should really learn to be more polite," Chelsea huffed, then called out, "MOM!"

Betty was cooking sausages in the kitchen, and the smell was already wafting through the house, making the dog's nose twitch.

"What can I do for you, officers?" Betty asked.

"We're here to search your house," Officer Sneaker repeated.

"Why?"

"We're looking for flying shoes and anyone from the notorious Foot family. Do you know anything about these shoes or, um, Foot folk?"

"Not really," Betty said calmly. "But feel free to look around."

She could see the officers were distracted by the smell of food. **"Would you officers like a sausage sandwich?"** she asked.

"Maybe one for the dog too?"

The officers hesitated.

"We're on duty," Officer Trainer reminded the others.

"We're due for a break," Officer Scarpin whispered.

"Quick look around and then have something to eat?"

"I AM starving," Officer Trainer said.

"And it's going to be a long day, with the awards tonight," Officer Sneaker added.

They quickly huddled together to discuss the options, then Officer Trainer asked, **"We need to know something very important first . . ."**

"Go on."

"Do you have any ketchup?"

"Of course," Betty assured them.

"And I'm vegetarian," Officer Scarpin told Betty.

"I have veggie bacon. I'll make some for you."

Then Officer Sneaker put up his hand.

"I'm gluten-free."

"No problem. I've got special bread."

"Vegan?" Officer Trainer added.

"Yup, got that covered too."

Betty had all the answers.

"Then it's settled. We'll stay."

The officers took the briefest of glances into every

room, easily missing the

Foot family hiding in

the bathroom. Which

was JUST what Betty

had wanted.

All clear.

The officers happily chowed down on breakfast and enjoyed every last mouthful. **"Lovely to meet you both. We'll remember the password next time, Chelsea!"** said Officer Trainer with a laugh.

"See you at the awards!" Officer Scarpin said.

"Yes, see you there!" Betty waved goodbye.

As soon as they left, Betty went to tell Ivor and the kids it was safe to come out. She found them in Chelsea's room—fast asleep. *They must be exhausted*, Betty thought, and left them to get some rest.

BERT had been working all night too, and NO NEWS wasn't going to be GOOD NEWS, Betty decided. **"Poor Bert. Making flying shoes in SUCH a short time is an impossible task. It will be a SHOE miracle if he succeeds."**

BERT had DONE IT! He'd followed all of Sally's instructions and made the flying shoes! Now he was busy testing them out, and so far the shoes were working perfectly. Bert couldn't stop LAUGHING and smiling as he zoomed around the room.

"THESE ARE THE BEST SHOES EVER! WE'RE GOING TO WIN THE GOLDEN SHOE AWARD NOW!"

Bert cheered.

He was so busy making so much noise that he didn't

hear the shop door being KICKED open or the PING

that meant someone had come in. And he missed the

THUD THUD THUD of VERY heavy footsteps until it

was too late . . .

"GIVE ME THOSE FLYING SHOES!"

a voice bellowed from the ground.

It was Wendy Wedge with Mr. Creeper. Bert hovered in the air.

"No, I won't. Get out of MY SHOP!" Bert said, still flying above their heads.

"THEY'RE MY SHOES now. COME DOWN, or things could get MESSY," Wendy ordered.

"No," Bert shot back.

"You will, OR ELSE." Wendy wasn't used to anyone disobeying her.

"I won't!" Bert shouted.

"You will!"

"I won't."

"YOU WILL TOO! GET them, Mr. Creeper—RIP them off his feet!" Wendy demanded.

Bert tucked his legs in tightly.

Mr. Creeper was tall—

but not THAT tall.

"STAY AWAY! I'm not coming DOWN!"
Bert told them, but the shoes' built-in voice
control heard Bert say **"DOWN"** and
obeyed the command. Bert floated toward
the ground, just enough for Mr. Creeper
to grab one of his ankles and drag
the shoes OFF his feet one by one.
Bert dropped to the floor with a THUMP.

"Bert, are you okay?" Wendy asked,
stepping OVER him to take the shoes.

**"You don't care—all you care about is
yourself,"** Bert said angrily.

"You know me so well." Wendy laughed.

Bert was FURIOUS. He sat there in a crumpled heap
and told Wendy exactly what he thought of her.

"YOU'RE a MEAN, spiteful, TERRIBLE person."

"Thank you. I try my best."

"It's not a compliment," Bert grunted through gritted
teeth.

Things were about to get EVEN WORSE

for Bert. Mr. Creeper spotted Sally's book.

"Ms. Wedge, THIS is the book Bert

dropped. All the instructions for making flying shoes

are in HERE." Mr. Creeper handed the book to Wendy.

The promotion was his now. He could feel it.

"HOW useful." Wendy flipped through a few pages,

then dropped it in her OVERSIZED bag.

"NO! You can't take that. It's Ivor's!"

Bert shouted at them.

"What's Ivor's is MINE," Wendy said smugly.

"It's a shoeTASTIC BOOK and I'm going to enjoy

using it. We would stay longer, Bert, but I have an

important GOLDEN SHOE AWARD to win

with these FLYING SHOES!" Wendy laughed, which

sounded like a MOOSE coughing.

"Ha! Ha! Ha! Ha!

Harrrrr Harrrrr!"

"And, Bert? Try to enjoy your little shop—you won't have it for much longer. But don't worry, you can always come and work for ME. Everyone does in the end."

Wendy smiled, then pushed a few of his nicest brogues onto the floor as she stomped out of the shop.

Bert groaned. All that hard work—for NOTHING!

Bert was SO angry.

It was WORSE than nothing . . .

It was all for WENDY WEDGE.

He'd had the flying shoes

ON HIS FEET.

What was he going to tell Betty and the kids now?

The truth: that Wendy was a ROTTEN, TERRIBLE, SELFISH, FIENDISH, SNEAKY, STOMPY, GRUMPY, THUMPY, HIDEOUS, NO GOOD, MEAN, WEDGEAWFUL* PERSON. And anything else he could think of.

*Foot note: He might have made that one up—but you get the idea.

DING-DONG

Size Thirty

The doorbell was ringing.

"That couldn't be the police again, could it?" Betty

peeked out the window. It wasn't the police. It was

Bert, and from the look on his face, he didn't have good

news. Betty let him in right away and said, **"Bert, don't**

worry, you did your best. It was a lot to expect. I'm

sorry the shoes didn't work."

She was trying her hardest to make him feel better.

"Oh, but they DID work!" Bert wailed as he walked

in. **"They worked perfectly. Then SHE of the WEDGE**

foot barged in with her horrible SIDEKICK and

STOLE them and Sally's book too. It's a DISASTER!"

Bert took a breath.

Just then, Chelsea ran in. **"Ivor, Ruby, and Bear are awake!"** she said

"Ivor's HERE?" Bert asked.

"I sure am," Ivor said, walking into the kitchen. He yawned and stretched.

"These fantastic children helped me escape! We were hiding— I must have fallen asleep. I feel so much better now."

"Well, I'm sorry, Ivor, but THAT's not going to last long. I made flying shoes last night. But Wendy Wedge stole them AND Sally's book.

"Wendy's got Mom's BOOK?" Ruby asked.

"I'm so sorry. They just TOOK it from me. We have to do something. She can't get away with it."

Bert was devastated.

(No one was happy with the Wendy Wedge situation.)

"If Wendy wins **THE GOLDEN SHOE AWARD**, she'll take over all the other towns and cities too. With her BIG clumpy wedges that have no SOUL," Ivor told them.

Bert nodded. **"I'll lose my shop for sure. We need a plan."**

The three of them continued discussing how terrible the situation was, and no one seemed to know what to do next. It was almost like Wendy had WON already.

"Hey, Ruby—remember you promised to tell me what you saw in Wendy's office? Now's a good time," said Bear.

Ruby jumped UP and started doing jumping jacks.

"Ruby, what are you doing?" Bear asked, confused.

"I'm just EXCITED!" said Ruby, jumping faster. "You won't believe it."

"Ruby, sit down. You're making everything wobble," Dad told her.

"Sorry, Ruby—please stop. I can't THINK if you JUMP." Bert still had his head in his hands.

"When I show you what I saw, Bert, you'll be jumping for joy too."

"I doubt that." Bert wasn't in a jumping mood.

"Okay, Ruby, we're listening," Dad said.

Ruby danced over to her bag and pulled out the camera wedge.

Ruby SET it to PLAY. **"Remember when I told you I HID under Wendy's bed?"**

"Yes, though I'm trying not to think about it," Dad told her.

"All of Shoe Town needs to SEE what kind of a person Wendy Wedge really is and what she's been up to," Ruby told them impressively.

"YES, Ruby," Bear chipped in. **"Get on with it."**

"Today everyone will be at THE GOLDEN SHOE AWARDS. And THAT'S where we HAVE to show THIS."

The video started and they all watched it OPENMOUTHED.

Dad broke into a BIG smile. Betty BEAMED. Chelsea grinned. Bear gave Ruby a high five.

"I'm ready to do some jumping jacks, if that's okay," Bert said.

Finally, it looked like they might be able to DO something about Wendy Wedge. No one was going to prison, and from the LOOKS on everyone's faces, things were going to change for the BETTER.

(At least, that's what they all HOPED.)

Size Thirty-One

"This is

AMAZING!

This is EVIDENCE that

Wendy has been up to NO good.

She won't have a WEDGE to

stand on," Dad told them, cheering

with relief. He had watched Ruby's

video ten times now, and every time it got better.

Ruby and Chelsea kicked off their wedges and were

dancing. Ruby called it the "SHOE shuffle."

Bert was still doing jumping jacks.

Betty cleared her throat. **"Sorry to break up the party—**
I need to go. I'll be backstage at THE GOLDEN
SHOE AWARDS, so wait for my signal to come to
the main CONTROL room. Ivor—you bring the camera.
Bert—you keep a lookout. Ruby, Bear, Chelsea—YOU
guys need to cause a distraction to keep the shoe police
away. Your DANCE would be perfect, or something
DRAMATIC. Right. Is everyone READY?" Betty wanted
to CHECK that EVERYONE was clear on the PLAN.

"We need a code name," said Bear.

"This is like a military operation," Bert agreed.

"How about Operation WEDGE?" Ivor suggested.

"WEDGE WARS!" Chelsea shouted.

"Wendy has too many things named after her
already," said Ruby. **"We have a name already—SHOE**
WARS?" she suggested.

"Nice!" Bert smiled.

"SHOE WARS it is, then,"
Betty said.

329

They all made a PINKIE PROMISE to STOP

the DREADED WENDY WEDGE

from EVER winning

THE GOLDEN SHOE AWARD

with FLYING SHOES.

(Shoo was excited to see the end of Wendy Wedge too.)

Size Thirty-Two

Wendy was in a SUPER-good mood that morning, with the flying shoes finally in her greedy grasp and **THE GOLDEN SHOE AWARDS** just hours away.

Paying an early visit to see Bert had been a GOOD move on her part. NOW she had a REAL pair of flying shoes. And they were FANTASTIC—just like she'd always dreamed they would be.

Wendy had tried them out around the apartment already, and she was looking forward to **THE GOLDEN SHOE AWARDS** EVEN MORE. Just thinking about it was making her feel all tingly. There was a knock at the door, and Wendy shouted, **"ENTER."**

Mr. Creeper shuffled in.

**"Is THAT what you're wearing for the awards?
I hope not"** was the first thing Wendy said to him.

"It's a new tie," Mr. Creeper told her.

"Did you keep the receipt?"
Wendy asked, not joking.

**"Was that why you wanted
to see me, Ms. Wedge?"** he asked.

"No. I wanted to tell you something exciting."

Mr. Creeper stood up taller. This was it; this was the
promotion he'd been waiting for. Not even Ivor Foot's
mysterious disappearance was going to RUIN this moment.

**"THINGS are going to be CHANGING around
here,"** Wendy told him. **"Everyone will want to own a
pair of flying shoes, so production and security has to
be STEPPED UP."**

"Yes, Ms. Wedge," he agreed.

"So," Wendy continued, a mean smile forming on her
lips. **"I'd like you to meet my NEW head of security."**

"I'm sorry?" Mr. Creeper thought he'd misheard.

333

A stern-looking woman with a scowl and mean eyes stomped in.

"Ms. Hobnail will be taking control of a lot of things here at WOW, including the development of the new range of flying wedges and ALL the security too. She's VERY experienced."

"Thank you, Ms. Wedge," she replied.

"But—but . . . that's MY job, Ms. Wedge," Mr. Creeper stammered.

"WAS your job. I've got plenty of other . . . things for you to do. Walter needs some training. Otherwise, HOW will he ever take over the family empire one day?"

Mr. Creeper didn't like the sound of this.

"It's a new era at WOW," Wendy continued. **"We'll need to start bringing in machines to make the flying shoes and get rid of a few miserable people."**

She stared at Mr. Creeper.

"But half the TOWN works here,"
Mr. Creeper reminded her.

"EXACTLY! Think of the money I'll save!"

Ms. Hobnail interrupted them. "Ms. Wedge, I have
that security footage you requested."

"Excellent. Mr. Creeper, FEAST your eyes on this."

 She clicked a remote. A video started
to play of WOW the night before.
Mr. Creeper watched in horror as the
Foot children snuck out of the building with their dad.

"Oh dear, my head of security fooled by children
in masks with sausages. Very AMATEUR, don't you
think, Mr. Creeper?" Wendy snarled.

"It wouldn't have happened on my watch," Ms.
Hobnail said.

"AND I had to find the shoes MYSELF!" Wendy
grimaced. "All this time, Ivor was lying to me, AND
those children are a PAIN. Those dogs
are refusing to eat anything other

335

THAN sausages now, HOPELESS. Plus, promotions

need to be EARNED, Mr. Creeper. For doing

something EXTRA—and you failed to find the

shoes. You're lucky Ms. Hobnail will be fixing your

mistakes and overseeing **THE GOLDEN SHOE**

AWARDS ceremony."

Mr. Creeper was defeated. **"Just tell me what you**

need, Ms. Wedge," he said quietly.

"Excellent, that's what I like to hear. You can bring

Walter down to my dressing room. Thank you, Mr.

Creeper. Let's not be SHOE-PID about this."

Wendy dismissed Mr. Creeper with a wave

of her hand, and then turned to her NEW

head of security.

"Now, Ms. Hobnail, we need to go over the

DETAILS for tonight. I want EVERYTHING to

be perfect."

Mr. Creeper slumped out of Wendy's office to find

Walter already there waiting (and tapping his foot).

"You took your time," Walter told Mr. Creeper rudely.

"Your mother wants you to wait in her dressing room. Let's go," he said wearily.

"That's boring. I have a better idea. YOU'RE always going into THAT room. WHAT'S in there? I want to know," Walter said, pointing at the door that led to Wendy's secret room full of creatures.

"You're not allowed to know or go in there. Your mother said so. It's locked," Mr. Creeper replied.

"NO WAY. I can do what I want," Walter said, then grabbed Mr. Creeper's badge and PUSHED past him.

Mr. Creeper wasn't in the mood to argue. He knew

Walter REALLY didn't like snakes. It was one of many

reasons Wendy kept the door locked, and it would serve

him right to be scared. Mr. Creeper decided to just wait

for Walter to come out . . .

. . . which

didn't take

very long.

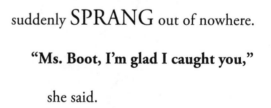

Size Thirty-Three

Betty left her house and set off for the WOW building. She'd present her MUSIC wedges at **THE GOLDEN SHOE AWARDS** just like she was supposed to, and try to PRETEND that everything was normal.

Wendy Wedge couldn't suspect a thing—and that wasn't going to be easy.

Betty was already feeling a little nervous. So the last thing she needed was anyone asking her difficult questions, like the shoe police or Mrs. Court . . . who suddenly SPRANG out of nowhere.

"Ms. Boot, I'm glad I caught you,"

she said.

"I'm in a bit of a hurry. I can't stop, Mrs. Court. I've got a lot going on. It's THE GOLDEN SHOE AWARDS today,"

Betty reminded her.

"Don't we all, Ms. Boot? I wanted to say good luck," Mrs. Court replied.

"Oh, thank you. Yes, I'll need it," Betty said, surprised.

"I'm assuming the Foot family is going too?" Mrs. Court asked.

"Ummm . . . maybe. I'm not really sure," said Betty vaguely.

"I think you DO know, Ms. Boot," Mrs. Court said, and gave her a look. Then she TWISTED the handle of her walking stick, clicked it in half, pulled out two flaps, pushed a few buttons, snapped out some tiny wheels, and the whole stick became a mini scooter. Mrs. Court ZOOMED OFF down the road.

"Bye, Mrs. Court. See you at the AWARDS?" Betty

called after her.

"YOU most certainly will!"

she called back.

The HUGE W building of Wedge Footquarters was lit up against the night sky. It looked SPECTACULAR. People from towns and cities all over were arriving for **THE GOLDEN SHOE AWARDS**.

TV presenters Kelly Kitten and Peter Peeptoe were broadcasting LIVE from the purple carpet. Their show, *Shoe Time*, could be seen on HUGE screens all around the World of Wedge venue.

"So the BIG question everyone is asking is: Will Shoehampton hold on to their record for the MOST GOLDEN SHOE AWARD wins ever? Or will rival cities Big Toehampton or Little Toehampton take the title? What do you think, Pete?"

"It's hard to call it right now, Kelly. Don't forget about the NEWcomers Stepford Town, and last year's second-place holders, Walking-on-Sea. Those 'Walk on Water' shoes they showed in the regional semi-finals were shoeTASTIC—don't you agree, Kelly?"

Kelly Kitten walked around the stage smiling and talking to the camera.

"Then there's Sneakerville, the city that's been quietly climbing the SHOE ladder. But THIS year is all about **Shoe Town**."

"You mean WEDGE Town, Kelly. Wendy Wedge changed the name," Pete corrected her.

"Of course she did. Everyone's wondering just WHAT Wendy Wedge at World of Wedge will be bringing to the party this time. **If she gets it right, Pete,** she could be on the **WEDGE OF GLORY!**"

"I'm resisting the URGE to sing, Kelly."

"Good job, Pete. And now let's go to a commercial break."

All of **Shoe Town** was buzzing with excitement about that evening's awards ceremony. Wendy Wedge had arrived in her private dressing room to get a little "quiet time" before her BIG AWARD moment.

Walter was already there and getting over his snake SHOCK by doing what HE thought was excellent tap dancing. This wasn't helping ease Wendy's stress.

After ten minutes (it felt like longer), Wendy asked him to stop.

"Walter, be a dear and do literally ANYTHING ELSE, will you?"

"But these tap shoes I found are fun," he told her.

"Not for me, they're not."

Walter frowned, folded his arms, and sulked.

"Walter, darling, you have to understand this is a very special time. I will be forever remembered, not just for WINNING THE GOLDEN SHOE AWARD, but for winning with never-before-seen flying shoes. I think this will be the VERY BEST moment of my ENTIRE LIFE!" Wendy sighed happily.

"Aside from when I was born," Walter added.

"That goes without saying." Wendy smiled (without actually saying it).

"You look very handsome, Walter," she told him so he'd stop sulking.

"What are these?" Walter asked, moving on to the

ELABORATE table of food.

"CHOUX buns. Help

yourself—oh, you

already have."

Manners weren't

a strong point for

Walter (or Wendy).

Walter took a plate of food, then flopped onto the

HUGE sofa. He turned on the W I D E-screen TV

to see that *Shoe Time* was coming live from outside the

WOW building. A picture of Wendy flashed across the

screen.

"LOOK, Mom. They're talking about you," Walter

told her.

"Of COURSE they are—I'm very important. Let

me listen." Wendy turned the volume UP.

"And we're BACK at this year's **GOLDEN SHOE AWARDS**, where the BEST **shoe towns** and cities will BATTLE it out to be crowned the WINNER! Wendy Wedge—and WEDGE TOWN—are hoping this is their year. What do you think, Kelly? Will WOW wow the judges?"

"Of course I will!"

Wendy shouted at the TV.

"Not sure, Pete. Wedge footwear can be a little bit on the STUFFY side. Sort of CLUMPY, LUMPY, sometimes even THUMPY. I mean, YOU KNOW when Wendy Wedge is on the prowl, right?"

"Ha! Yes, Kelly, she makes an IMPACT, that's for sure!"

At this point, Wendy turned the sound OFF.

"Awwww, I was watching that!" Walter complained.

"They're FOOLS! What do THEY know about fabulous FOOTWEAR? NOTHING! That's what. I'll show THEM, and anyone who EVER doubted me."

Wendy sneered.

Walter kept watching the silent television screen. As the camera panned over the huge crowd of people arriving, he shuffled closer to the TV and peered at the screen.

"Mom, LOOK! It's the Foot family and Bert Brogue in some . . . WEIRD disguises. I can spot them a mile away."

Wendy came over and squinted at the screen.

"Oh, look at that! It is! How nice of them to come as a group. It will be so much easier to arrest them ALL TOGETHER. I'll let the NEW guards know where to find them—RIGHT NOW. VERY good job, Walter."

Wendy rubbed her hands together in anticipation.

"Thank you, Mom. I might do another quick tap dance." Walter smiled.

"Absolutely NOT," Wendy told him quickly.

There was a knock at the door. It was Officer T-Bar

coming to tell Wendy the awards were about to begin.

"THIS is MY MOMENT to SOAR. I am ready for my CLOSE-UP,"

Wendy said dramatically.

She stood in front of the mirror to check her pose

and practice her acceptance speech. She didn't need to

remember a list of names, because she wasn't planning

on thanking anyone.

Walter shoved more food into his mouth and tap-

danced behind his mother as she THUMPED her way

backstage.

Tap, tap, tap, tappety-tap . . .

THUMP.

THUMP.

THUMP.

THUMP.

(Everybody could tell that

Wendy was on her way.)

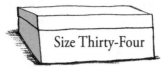

Size Thirty-Four

"**D**o you think anyone will recognize us?" Ruby whispered to Bear.

"**I don't think so,**" Bear said, and slipped in his fake teeth.

"**They look good on you!**" Ruby laughed.

"**Can you still speak?**" Chelsea asked.

"**Naw wearly,**" Bear tried.

"**Even better.**" Ruby smiled and flicked back her long black Halloween witch's wig. Along with the fake teeth, Bear wore a floppy hat, and Chelsea had on STAR glasses and a cape. Bert's fake mustache and spiky wig were a triumph of disguise. And Ivor's curly wig looked almost real.

They joined the line to go in. A guard that Ivor didn't
recognize stopped them. He spoke to Bear.

"How old are you? No kids allowed in on their own."

Bear shook his head. He couldn't talk or else his teeth
would fall out.

"They're all with me," Ivor said as confidently as he
could.

"Okay. Do you know where you're going?" the guard
asked Bear, who opened his mouth to answer.
The guard looked horrified as the teeth
dropped into his hand.

"Oops!"

There were signs EVERYWHERE that said:

NO PHONES OR CAMERAS—OR ELSE!

Ivor had snuck in two cameras—by wearing them! It was a HUGE relief that he hadn't been stopped. Now that they were safely inside the grounds of WOW, Ivor took them off—he was just in his socks, but that didn't matter. He gave one of the camera wedges to Ruby and Bear to hold.

"Put on the wrist control and we can keep in touch," he told them. **"Now you guys head to the front and keep a lookout for Betty's signal."**

"We'll head to the control room, and once YOU give us the all clear, then it's SHOE WARS all the way," Bert reminded everyone. **"Ruby, why are you laughing?"**

"Sorry." Ruby giggled. **"It's just your mustache. It looks really funny."**

Ivor and Bert headed to the control room while Ruby, Bear, and Chloe mingled with the crowds, trying not to stick out—but failing.

None of this went unnoticed by Ms. Hobnail and her

NEW security team. They had already ZOOMED in on the odd collection of people.

"Focus on that group . . ." she said. "They're UP to something. They could be the Foot gang Ms. Wedge is looking for."

"Shall we arrest them now?" Security Officer Plimsoll asked.

"Not yet—let's keep watching. Ms. Wedge wants to wait for the right moment," Ms. Hobnail said in a very threatening way.

Meanwhile, Betty had a PROBLEM.

Her badge had stopped working, and the control room was now surrounded by NEW security guards. It was going to be impossible to get in, and Betty HAD to warn Ivor and Bert. Finding another way to get their video on the big screen wasn't going to be easy. Backstage, Betty paced around her coworkers, wondering what to do next. Ms. Hobnail appeared. **"There's been a change of plan. None of you are needed anymore—except for YOU, Betty Boot. You stay RIGHT here."**

"WHY me?" Betty asked. **"Just do as I say . . ."** Ms. Hobnail told her. She was in a bad mood.

"But who's going to represent Shoe— I mean, WEDGE TOWN? We've ALL worked so hard on these SHOWSTOPPING wedges," Phillip Flop told Ms. Hobnail (like she cared).

"STUPID question—Wendy Wedge, of COURSE. She's guaranteed to win, and you all will just make things more complicated. Betty Boot, don't move a muscle," Ms. Hobnail snarled, then gestured to the security guards to keep an EYE on her.

Betty didn't like the way things were going. She waited until Ms. Hobnail had left before making her way to the side of the stage.

"Exciting!" Betty said, trying to convince the guards that she was just being curious. Then she peeked around the BIG screen to see a HUGE crowd of expectant people, who were all waiting for the awards to begin. Thanks to their choices of disguises, Betty spotted Ruby, Bear, and Chelsea immediately. (They weren't exactly blending in.)

Betty waved furiously, trying to attract their attention.

"Look, there's Betty." Bear waved back.

THE GOLDEN
SHOE AWARD

"That's the signal," Chelsea said. Ruby turned on her

wrist control. **"Ivor and Bert, Shoe Wars is a GO."**

The lights went down and spotlights circled the WHOLE venue. Thumping music blared, and the crowd went quiet, except for one person who couldn't stop coughing (there's always one). A spotlight shone on each judge as they were introduced.

They waved to the audience as they CHEERED. Finally, the camera went to . . .

THE GOLDEN SHOE AWARD.

There was a BIG GASP, and the audience clapped some more. The award was a stylish GOLD shoe on a stand under a glass dome. The announcer boomed,

"So, now that you've met the judges, let's get the show started. I've just been told there's a small change to the schedule . . ."

"... WEDGE TOWN will be represented EXCLUSIVELY by ... the one and ONLY Wendy Wedge!"

There was a light ripple of applause. (But not much. Wendy was not very popular.)

"Sit back and enjoy the spectacle that is

THE GOLDEN SHOE AWARDS!"

Flashing lights and wandering spotlights hit the shoewalk,

and the award began to GLOW.

"INTRODUCING OUR FIRST CONTESTANT

FROM **SHOECASTLE.**

THIS YEAR THEY BRING YOU

THE SUSHI SHOE—

A REVOLVING CONVEYOR

BELT OF TASTY TREATS

CONTAINED IN

A COOL

ENVIRONMENT.

STYLISH FOOD

FOR YOUR FEET."

"Next up: THE SHOE GARDEN.
A FEAST FOR THE EYES, SUPER GOOD FOR
THE ENVIRONMENT, AND COMPLETE WITH
A BUILT-IN WATERING SYSTEM. IT REGROWS
EVERY FEW WEEKS. IT'S A REALLY LEAF-
TASTIC SHOE."

367

"THERE'S NOTHING SMALL ABOUT THESE TENNIS SHOES FROM **LITTLE TOEHAMPTON—** THEY AUTOMATICALLY MOVE TO WHERE THE BALL IS, AND THE GRAB HANDS MEAN NEVER HAVING TO PICK UP A BALL AGAIN, EVER! AND HERE COME THE EXTRA-SPEEDY, SOUPED-UP CAR SHOES WITH **HOT WHEELS!** I hope they're SUPPOSED to be on fire!"

"YOU'LL NEVER WANT TO TAKE

OFF THESE BOOK SHOES FROM

BIG ᴛᴏᴇʜᴀᴍᴘᴛᴏɴ,

WITH A COMPACT READING LIGHT AND

AUTOMATIC PAGE TURNING TOO."

So far the display of shoes looked EXCITING. The

judges were feverishly taking notes on and scoring each

shoe. There were cries of "Oooooooooooh" for

SNEAKERVILLE'S endless waterfall shoes . . .

"THE SHOES THAT COOL YOUR FEET! YOU'LL

ALWAYS HAVE WATER ON TAP."

Then there were "AHHHHHHHs" when the

HOVER SHOES floated down the shoewalk—

until they **BURST**

and deflated.

(Deflating the judges too.)

The rechargeable PHONE shoes were sort of underwhelming.

But everyone loved the chameleon shoes.

The OCTI shoes STUCK to the side of the WALL in an excellent demonstration of their SUCTION power.

(The invisible shoes fooled NO ONE.)

With the awards in FULL SWING, Ivor and Bert made their way to the control room. **"Uh-oh, this isn't going to work,"** Ivor whispered.

There were GUARDS EVERYWHERE.

"What's plan B, then?" Bert asked.

Ivor thought for a moment. **"Storm the stage?"**

Bert looked shocked. **"Really?"**

"Okay, maybe not. We could CUT the power and project the video directly from the CAMERA SHOE on to the big screen," Ivor said. **"Just like Ruby suggested."**

Bert agreed, and plan B it was.

Setting off to locate the central FUSE box backstage, Bert and Ivor tried their BEST to keep a low profile. All this time, Ms. Hobnail and the security team were still following them with their cameras—VERY closely.

"I've seen enough—arrest them!" she announced to ALL her security officers.

Ms. Hobnail checked the time—Wendy Wedge was expected to be on the SHOEWALK very soon. Ms. Hobnail was pleased that everything was under control.

"Ms. Hobnail." One eagle-eyed security guard got her attention. **"We've detected unusual activity in the WOW building, and it's heading straight toward THE GOLDEN SHOE AWARDS**—at GREAT SPEED."

"Let me take a look." Ms. Hobnail ordered them to zoom in and FREEZE-FRAMED several of the cameras.

"Is that what I think it is?" a security guard asked in an ALARMED tone.

"YES, I think it is. WE ALL need to stay CALM! I've GOT this," Ms. Hobnail shouted,

while NOT sounding very

calm at all.

Bert moved into position to TURN off the power while Ivor hid by the side of the stage. He was POISED to LEAP into ACTION and show EVERYONE what a HUGE LIAR Wendy Wedge was.

Bert opened the gray box and put his hands on the red lever, ready to turn OFF the power . . .

When a voice behind him said, **"Don't MOVE a MUSCLE."**

Bert froze—he'd been CAUGHT red-handed.

"Look at your FEET," the voice said, and this time Bert recognized who it was.

"Betty?" said Bert, then he glanced down.

SNAKES!

Bert stayed as still as he could. **"OH NO!"**

It was FAR too dangerous to turn off the power now.

"Stay calm—everything will be fine. They'll be gone soon," Betty told him as, one after the other, the snakes slithered across his feet.

Betty was right, and the snakes soon slithered off. But it was too late. **"Hold it right there,"** came a cold voice. It was one of Ms. Hobnail's guards. **"You are ALL under arrest."**

Hissssssssssss

After a few moments, the snakes were gone, but it was too late: The guards had spotted Betty and Bert and arrested them both.

While Bert was FOOT-deep in poisonous snakes, back with *Shoe Time*, the camera had cut to Kelly Kitten and Peter Peeptoe, who were PROJECTED onto the BIG screen. It was clear they had been told to fill in the time.

"Hello, looks like there's a little delay before we can get to see anything else. Isn't that right, Pete?"

"We've seen some SUPERB shoes, haven't we, Kelly?"

"Yes, we have, Pete. I wonder if they'd look as good on my size-nine feet?"

"Wow, you have bigger feet than I thought, Kelly."

"What's wrong with being a size nine, Pete?"

"Nothing at all. We're STILL looking for the shoe that's really going to KNOCK our socks off, right, Kelly?"

"Nine is a normal foot size—I'm just saying. I mean, WHAT size are you?"

"I think we're going to another BREAK . . . Back in five," Pete said.

"Nine is a good size," Kelly muttered.

Meanwhile Wendy had put on her flying shoes and was ready to make her grand **ENTRANCE.**

The one she'd DREAMED about for so many years!

She waited . . .   And waited . . .

BUT there was some kind of HOLDUP.

"What's going ON?"

Wendy demanded.

"Why is it taking so long?"

Mr. Creeper was standing next to her, and he shrugged.

"You'd better ask your NEW head of security. Here she comes now."

Ms. Hobnail waddled over to see them. She looked serious.

"Ms. Hobnail, there BETTER be a good reason for this DELAY."

"Ms. Wedge, there is. We have a VERY BIG problem."

"I AGREE—I SHOULD be holding the award by now. Let's get started, shall we?"

"We can't, Ms. Wedge. I'm afraid we might have to EVACUATE and ABANDON the whole awards show for safety reasons," she told Wendy.

"WHAT ARE YOU TALKING ABOUT? Don't be ridiculous. Mr. Creeper, tell her—I'm not leaving."

Mr. Creeper hesitated. "Ms. Wedge, maybe you should listen . . ."

"I'M NOT GOING ANYWHERE— just figure it out. I've got an award to WIN!" Wendy shouted at them, and prepared herself to walk onstage.

Ms. Hobnail tried again. "Ms. Wedge, our security cameras have spotted LOTS of RARE, POISONOUS SNAKES on the loose. We've found some backstage. The rest could be anywhere. We don't want the situation to get out of control."

Wendy ROLLED her eyes.

"ARE you kidding me? WHAT KIND OF FOOL LET THOSE SNAKES OUT in the FIRST place? They're only a tiny bit poisonous, by the way. Who's the IDIOT who WASN'T PAYING ATTENTION? I'LL NEVER TRUST them EVER AGAIN!" Wendy bellowed, and STARED at Mr. Creeper. But Mr. Creeper had NO intention of taking the blame.

"It wasn't ME; it was WALTER!" he squeaked.

Walter FRANTICALLY denied everything.

"Mr. Creeper LET me go in! IT'S NOT MY FAULT! IF I'd KNOWN there were snakes in those TANKS, I'd NEVER have opened them UP! I was JUST LOOKING. I HATE snakes!"

But everybody could tell he was lying—even Wendy.

"OH. I see."

She did a good job of hiding her FURY.

"We have to shut down the awards,

Ms. Wedge," Ms. Hobnail repeated.

"ABSOLUTELY NOT! Just keep a lookout! Once

I've won the award, you can do what you want. And

if anyone gets bitten, just take them to the hospital.

They won't DIE," Wendy said.

"But . . . but Sally Sandal did . . ."

Mr. Creeper pointed out.

"I didn't know she'd been BITTEN. No one did

until it was too late. Moving ON!"

Wendy took a step toward the stage. "Please don't,

Ms. Wedge!" cried Ms. Hobnail.

"If you think I'm going to give UP!" shrieked Wendy,

and at that, the flying shoes KICKED into ACTION.

There was nothing

anyone could do to stop her.

"**BACK LIVE** at **THE GOLDEN SHOE AWARDS.**

Looks like we're all ready to go! NEXT UP—it's Wendy Wedge. AND size nine is a perfectly normal size shoe to have, just saying."

"We hear you, Kelly. **THE GOLDEN SHOE AWARD** is really HEATING up now. I think I can hear her coming already . . ."

A single spotlight shone on the empty stage. Wendy was about to make her entrance . . .

Size Thirty-Five

Ruby, Chelsea, and Bear watched as Wendy

WOBBLED her way onto the shoe stage.

"Are those the flying shoes?" Chelsea whispered.

"I think so," replied Bear.

"Why isn't she flying, then?"

Bear squinted at Wendy, who hovered for a few

seconds and then dropped back down. "The wings

look . . . stuck."

The people in the crowd weren't impressed either.

They began to laugh as Wendy stumbled around.

"What's she doing?" someone yelled.

"Wendy gets the award for the dullest shoes—

AGAIN!" sneered another.

There was still no sign of Betty, Bert, or Dad, and Ruby was starting to wonder if something had gone wrong.

"COME ON!" a man bravely shouted out.

Wendy shot him a GLARE. Then, through gritted teeth, she hissed: **"I'll show you all . . . SHOES UP!"**

The two wings unfolded properly and began to flutter. Wendy gradually LIFTED off the ground and the audience GASPED as she began to fly over their heads.

Ruby made a face. **"Dad should be up there flying, not HER."**

But where were the grown-ups? Time was running out.

Wendy went from side to side,
upside down, and around the heads
of the crowd. She even got a bit carried
away and did a LOOP-THE-LOOP. Then, just
when everything was going SO well, she
JOLTED to one side.

Then to the other.

Oww!

Agh!

"SHOES DOWN.

SHOES DOWN!"

Wendy managed to even the shoes out, and she
floated back down and landed with a curtsy.

With the judges busy writing
down notes and scores, Wendy
SOAKED up the applause, then
STOMPED back up the shoewalk.

As soon as she got backstage, she was MORE

than delighted to see that Ms. Hobnail

had arrested Betty, Bert, and Ivor.

AT LAST!

"Wasn't I FANTASTIC?" she said to them. **"You

HAVE TO STAY and watch me get the award. It's the

LEAST I can do."** Wendy was LOVING this (too much).

"You can't keep us prisoner forever," Ivor told her.

"That's what YOU think," Wendy snapped.

**"Mom, you FLEW really well—except for the ending

when we ALL thought you MESSED up and Mr.

Creeper was laughing,"** said Walter, who was a snitch.

"I wasn't," Mr. Creeper said.

"You were." He was *such* a snitch.

"THE GOLDEN SHOE AWARD will be

yours, Ms. Wedge,"** Mr. Creeper reassured Wendy. At

the same time, he was keeping his eyes on the ground for

anything slithery.

Wendy chose to IGNORE them.

"WHEN are they going to GIVE me my award?" she asked impatiently. An assistant ran up.

"Ms. Wedge, the judges' scores are in. Would you like to take your place?"

"My place is NEXT to the PRIZE. I can get it faster then, before Ms. Grumpy Chops over there tries to stop everything." Wendy elbowed her way past the other contestants and casually leaned right NEXT to **THE GOLDEN SHOE AWARD**.

"WE ALL know there's only ONE winner!"

Wendy announced.

The judges tried not to be intimidated and gave out the prizes for:

Best Special Effect, Best Use of Materials, Best Sound, Most Ecological.

"For goodness' SAKE!" Wendy muttered, and ROLLED her eyes.

Kelly Kitten and Peter Peeptoe had joined them now to PRESENT the winner.

"FINALLY, Kelly, we're at the main event. The award to end all awards. THIS is the moment we've all been waiting for!"

"That's right, Pete.

THE GOLDEN SHOE AWARD

this year goes to . . ."

"We'll be BACK after this commercial break!"

Have a GREAT holiday—
but don't forget your
TRAVEL INSURANCE.

Terms and conditons apply wiahuhfoubaifbsd
ghe euer hgushgowihduwhfiuqehgiwugehtiwugtjaofhweuh giiwui annagjfhiegfilwru iytg
aliorugtjaiwsgui4t:iwgUEP:BE SVOSKBS HPOHEOPH PIHEOHPGO WOIHEOEGRH
OIHEO BTUHEOHPFBDIPHIW GERIWOHPOIH OI HOFHIEOHGOWIHEGOHWEGOR
LEHIGOWIHROWOBGIGWHIRGOAO WERSGOWGROFHOWEHPFDFWE BOFHHWOIE
RGO IWUGERIWUEGP IGUGEFIQUEFIUEIWUEIGUWBUI NFGW RIEGOWHEGOWIHGH OIW
URGIWUGGIWEGOWHGOWHIE JGJHEOHJF FIHEIHO hoihge eihohgo ihjipojpeoppg

MMMMMMMMM, TEA . . .

When you're feeling stressed,
put your feet up and pour
yourself a lovely cup of TEA
. . . and RELAX.

"And we're back! Are you ready for a VERY special announcement?"

"GET ON WITH IT!" Wendy

shrieked from the side, then remembered she was on TV.

"Someone's excited! Well, the WINNER of this year's GOLDEN SHOE AWARD is . . ."

"Wendy Wedge from Wedge Town, formerly known as Shoe Town, with her amazing, incredible, never-before-seen flying shoes!"

Wendy SNATCHED **THE GOLDEN SHOE AWARD** and CLUTCHED it tightly so no one could take it away.

"AT LAST! It's mine, ALL MINE!" she cried out. Then Wendy's eyes narrowed, and she made a speech. Not a nice one either.

"It's about TIME I got this award. It's SO well deserved! I have no one to THANK but myself. BUT I have a lot of people to blame for almost RUINING my moment. It's not been easy to concentrate. There's a bunch of people HERE we have to ARREST! Bring them OUT."

Ms. Hobnail decided to ENJOY her moment of glory and shoved Bert, Betty, and Ivor onto the shoewalk.

The crowd had no idea what was going on, but Ruby, Bear, and Chelsea knew EXACTLY what was happening!

(It was NOW or never to show their video on the BIG screen.)

"These TERRIBLE people have been PLOTTING against ME. And they're not the ONLY ones!" Wendy spun around and GLARED into the crowd.

"**Chief Inspector Slingback, ARREST those funny-looking kids. Don't think I didn't SEE you there the WHOLE time!**" Wendy said, pointing at Ruby, Bear, and Chelsea. The spotlight landed on a small man with a mustache.

"**NO, not HIM! THEM—YES!**"

The crowd began to mutter. No one liked the idea of chasing kids.

"Listen to ME—THOSE kids are CRIMINALS. They ruined my sign and TERRORIZED my son with RED paint. And this man HERE . . ." (She pointed to Ivor.) ". . . BROKE WEDGE LAW. He's been arrested for the possession of illegal SLIPPERS!"

"THESE two helped him. NO ONE IN WEDGE

TOWN SHOULD OWN A PAIR OF THOSE

TERRIBLE THINGS. SLIPPERS ARE BANNED!

ANYONE WHO OWNS THEM HAS TO BE

ARRESTED!"

The crowd began to **LAUGH**. (A lot.)

Wendy was NOT happy at all.

At that moment, Ruby flipped on the camera, which projected the video behind Wendy. Inspector Slingback made a grab for her, but Bear fended him off. Chelsea threw some sausages at the dogs to create some extra chaos.

Look OUT!

Woof Woof!

"DID you hear me?
ILLEGAL slippers!
IT'S SHOCKING!"

Wendy shouted again, and everyone screeched with laughter even more.

Ha! HA! HA! HA! Ha!

Ha! HA! HA! HA! Ha!

On the screen BEHIND Wendy Wedge were her feet wearing her fluffy pink slippers with pom-poms. The timing couldn't have been more perfect.

"Don't LAUGH—you have NO idea WHAT they've done!" Wendy shouted back.

Ivor tried to BREAK free to help his kids. **"Take your hands off my kids. YOU'RE the one in trouble,"** he told her bravely.

"NONSENSE! Your DELINQUENT children vandalized my sign and dropped PAINT onto my POOR WALTER, who needs an apology NOW. Say SORRY to MY son PUBLICLY, you FOUL FOOTS," Wendy shouted, then called for Walter to join her.

"Mom, I think the crowd is laughing at you," Walter had to explain to his mother as the laughing got louder.

The shoe police tried to GRAB the children, but they

wriggled FREE.

NOW the whole country was watching everything

unfold LIVE on *Shoe Time.*

Wendy turned then and saw the film behind her.

Ruby's wig

"It's a fake!" she screamed. **"Part

of a terrible smear campaign!"**

Ruby wasn't having any of it.

She jumped up onstage and told everyone the TRUTH.

"It's NOT FAKE! I saw her wearing slippers!" she

told the crowd. Then Bear and Chelsea joined her.

**"Wendy Wedge keeps SNAKES and other

RARE creatures to make SECRET WEDGES

from. WE SAW them!"** Bear added.

**"NONSENSE! That's a lot of OLD shoe leather.

Don't listen to these CHILDREN!"** Wendy said, forcing

a smile.

Now Chelsea joined them. **"LOOK, everyone—here are all of Wendy's secrets!"**

Wendy turned around and SAW for herself THE HORROR of all her SECRETS on the screen. The bugs. The snakes. The SLIPPERS.

"STOP THAT FAKE VIDEO RIGHT NOW! HOW did this happen?" Wendy looked at Ms. Hobnail—and around desperately for Mr. Creeper too.

"THOSE snakes on the loose are poisonous, and they are the SAME snakes that bit and KILLED my Sally Sandal!" Ivor told Wendy angrily.

"It wasn't MY fault a SNAKE escaped! Sally was in the WRONG place at the WRONG time. So NOT my fault. AND those kids FAKED that video! It's a load of FOOTSWALLOP, isn't it, Chief Inspector Slingback? And, Mr. Creeper, you'll stick up for me?"

But there was no answer. Desperately,

Wendy tried to FLY AWAY.

"Not so fast!" Ivor shouted, and tried

to GRAB her foot, but she slipped AWAY!

OFF she flew over everyone's heads, trying hard to

hold on to her **GOLDEN SHOE AWARD**.

(Which wasn't easy.)

Ruby, Bear, Chelsea, Ivor, Betty, and Bert watched her

helplessly from the stage. She was getting away with it!

Then, out of NOWHERE

from the crowd, a thin rope SHOT up

and wrapped around Wendy's ankles, tying them

together. Like a FISH on a hook, she was dragged down

to the ground.

"GET OFF ME!" she yelped.

The crowd parted, and at the END of the rope,

pulling Wendy Wedge to the ground, was . . .

...MRS. COURT!

"Is that YOU, Mrs. Court?" Ruby gasped.

Bear and Chelsea had their mouths

open in amazement.

Mrs. Court ignored

them. She calmly finished

pulling Wendy Wedge to earth

with her special walking stick.

Wendy looked surprised to be

caught as well. Then a

group of official-

looking police

stepped onto

the stage.

"WHAT do you think you're DOING?" Wendy shouted.

"WENDY WEDGE, MY NAME IS CYBIL COURT, and I'M FROM THE FEDERAL FOOTWEAR INVESTIGATIONS TEAM. YOU ARE UNDER ARREST FOR SO MANY THINGS I BARELY KNOW WHERE TO BEGIN. So let's start with THESE:

1. USING RARE, PROTECTED CREATURES
   TO MAKE WEDGES.
2. ILLEGALLY KEEPING POISONOUS SNAKES.
3. NOT KEEPING YOUR SNAKES SECURE,
   so they escaped and killed Sally Sandal.
4. MAKING UP YOUR OWN LAWS. There's
   NOTHING wrong with SLIPPERS.
5. KIDNAPPING YOUR WORKERS and
   threatening CHILDREN.
6. NOT PAYING YOUR TAXES.

I COULD GO ON."

Mrs. Court sent her officers out to arrest Chief Inspector Slingback too, for taking BRIBES from Wendy and generally being a TERRIBLE inspector.

Mrs. Court turned to Ivor. **"I've been WATCHING your house for some time, Mr. Foot, as part of my wider investigation into Ms. Wedge. I saw the flying shoes, I kept away Mr. Creeper with my special DART blower, and I wanted to keep your flying shoes safe for you, so I TOOK them before Mr. Creeper had a chance to steal them. HERE they are, Mr. Foot."**

She took them out of her bag and handed them over.

"**Mrs. Court? YOU had them!**" Ivor said, gratefully

taking back Sally's shoes.

"**Mrs. Court has saved the day!**" Bear cheered.

"**HOORAY for Mrs. Court!**" Ruby yelled, excited to

have an opportunity to admire her walking stick up close.

"**This belongs to you too,**" Mrs. Court said, handing

Sally Sandal's book to Ruby and Bear. "**Look after it.**

It's clearly something VERY special. I wouldn't mind

wearing a few of those shoes, IF you ever make them."

411

Ruby, Bear, and Chelsea were speechless. NOSY old Mrs.

Court was the last person they'd expected to SAVE the day.

Bert walked up onstage and TOOK the shoes off

Wendy.

"Officers, and the Shoe

Award Jury, I think you'll

ALSO find Wendy Wedge

STOLE these shoes from ME. They were made thanks

to the instructions of the wonderful Sally Sandal."

Wendy knew the GAME was up, so she tried another

tactic.

"All I've ever tried to DO was be nice to people,

GIVE everyone a JOB, and look after everyone in

WEDGE—um, **Shoe Town**, ASK Mr. Creeper! HE's

about to get a BIG promotion. MR. CREEPER, you

can tell them how kind I am, can't you?"

If Wendy THOUGHT Mr. Creeper was going to STICK up for her, she was WRONG.

Mr. Creeper stepped forward. **"Wendy has done ALL the things you accuse her of. I'm ashamed to say I've helped her. I can give you all the evidence you need. I'd rather see those creatures FREE in the wild than on someone's FEET."**

He then turned to Wendy. **"I'm tired of being treated badly, Ms. Wedge. You've been an absolute nightmare to work for."**

(And that was an understatement.)

Wendy was SHOCKED.

"AND you need to say NO to your son once in a while and READ stories to him a lot more."

Mr. Creeper finished his speech and felt nothing but RELIEF!

"Mother, what's going to happen to ME now? Because I WOULD actually like to have stories read to me," Walter piped up.

"Well, that's not going to happen now, IS it?" Wendy snapped at her son as she was dragged away by the police. **"I'll make sure MY lawyers get me out. In the meantime, your uncle Wilberforce Wedge will have to look after you."**

"BUT I barely KNOW him," Walter whined.

"What's to know? He was our parents' favorite child. He always laughed at me,

made me feel useless, blah blah. He'll look after you. He can't make you WORSE than you already are."

"MOTHER, how can you say that?" Walter cried.

"Mr. Creeper's right. I should have said no to you more. So, I'll start now. Can you stay with someone else? NO! TOUGH."

Wendy thought she'd try ONE last thing to get RID of all these annoying people around her.

She called HER DOGS.

"LEFT and RIGHT, GET me out of here! SEIZE them!"

The dogs glanced up, but they didn't feel like moving much. Not after all those sausages.

Wendy sighed. It was over.

One of the judges tried to wrestle **THE GOLDEN SHOE AWARD** away from her.

"BUT that's mine! I won it—you GAVE it to me!"
she wailed.

"Not anymore, Wendy Wedge. We're awarding it to
Bert Brogue, who MADE the flying shoes."

Bert came up to take it and turned to the cameras.

"Thank you. BUT this doesn't belong to me, it belongs
to Ivor and to Ruby and Bear Foot and to their
mother, Sally Sandal, who designed the shoes. I just
followed her instructions."

Bert handed the award to the Foot family.

They were all smiling for the cameras and celebrating,

when someone in the crowd shouted . . .

"SNAKE! SNAKE!"

Which wasn't an insult to Wendy BUT THE REAL

THING! AGGHHHHHHHHH!

There was MAD PANIC as everyone ran in all

different directions. One of the snakes was slithering UP

the shoewalk—right toward the stage!

IVOR FROZE. He had a deep-seated FEAR of snakes.

Bert threw his shoe at it, which only made it

MADDER.

Then Ruby sPRANG into action.

She GRABBED Mrs. Court's walking stick and

pointed it at the snake, while pressing ALL the buttons.

A SHARP FORK shot out of the top and PINNED the

snake down.

"Don't go near it!" Mrs. Court shouted.

The snake was starting to work its way

OUT of the prong, when suddenly

Shoo the cat appeared from

backstage and POUNCED on it.

Shoo held the snake down long enough for Officer

Slingback and Officer Trainer to arrive with a BIG

shoebox and take it away safely.

The crowd began to cheer and clap their hands in

relief.

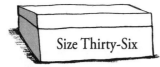

Size Thirty-Six

"It's been QUITE a show! We've had flying shoes—those were A M A Z I N G. I want a pair of those right now! Don't you, Pete?"

"I really do, Kelly. What I don't want to see again is a SNAKE. Here are the WINNERS of **THE GOLDEN SHOE AWARD** to tell us all about what happened today.

"Ivor, what can you tell us? Ivor?"

"Hi, I'm Ruby. Dad's in SHOCK right now. He doesn't like snakes. This is my friend, Chelsea. She lives next door."

"Hi! My mom's over there. Her name's Betty, and she rescued Ruby and Bear when Wendy was trying to get them. We had a sleepover—and I gave them Mom's badge to get into World of Wedge," Chelsea said.

"She did and THAT helped us get into the secret place where the CREATURES were. AND this is my brother, Bear."

"Hi! My sister talks a lot. THAT'S Bert. He MADE the shoes from a book that our mom wrote. Bert, come and say hello."

"Bert, you must be proud of making the shoes too?" Kelly Kitten asked.

"Well, it's really Sally and Ivor's dream. I hope we can make more and sell them in MY shop—Bert's Brogues—which will be staying OPEN FOREVER now!" Bert said, and did a little dance on live TV.

Then Ivor unfroze and joined in, and so did Betty and the kids too.

"What a happy ending to a VERY eventful day. The judges awarded **THE GOLDEN SHOE AWARD** to Ivor Foot and Sally Sandal in the end. So let's leave you with the whole FOOT family and their friends dancing!

Keep smiling.

"Until next year! It's Kelly Kitten and Peter Peeptoe saying BYE for now from

Wedge Town—I mean **SHOE TOWN!**"

"Hey, Bear . . . do you think Mom would like my shoe shuffle dance?" Ruby wanted to know.

"She would!" Bear said.

"Your mom would be very proud of us all . . ." Dad added, and gave them a hug. "It's all in the foot action, kids—see?" he added, and joined in.

So, I know what you're wondering now . . .

What happened after Wendy was dragged to Shoe Prison?

Left and Right went to live with Mr. Creeper, who, in exchange for providing evidence against Wendy, was given a shortened sentence, after completing some community service picking up litter.

Mrs. Court's walking stick came in very handy for that.

He eventually got to go on a well-earned vacation.

(The dogs went too.)

Walter was sent to stay with Wendy's brother, Wilberforce

Wedge, who had refused to come to **Shoe Town** to look

after him.

(The truth was, HE had been in prison for years. He was let out for

good behavior just as Wendy arrived, but that's another story.)

Bert kept his shop open and started to make flying brogues.

The World of Wedge was renamed WOOF, World of Original Footwear. Betty and Ivor took over design and production at WOOF. They created and sold the type of weird and wonderful shoes that Ivor and Sally used to make in their shop, using many of Sally Sandal's original designs. Some of the money from the shoes went toward looking after the RARE creatures and bugs and keeping them safe. Even the snakes.

WOOF did SO well that all the **Shoebox** houses were able to have second-story additions so they weren't so tiny anymore.

Ruby and Bear got their OWN ROOMS, which

ended their arguments about who was the messiest. There

was more space, which meant Chelsea could sleep over

as well.

Bear still liked sliced peaches with lemon curd and was writing a lot of stories now. He already had plenty of material to work with (his family's war with Wendy, just to start).

Ruby tried making a walking stick like Cybil Court's. Hers was painted with lightning bolts, and she mostly used it to annoy Bear.

Pretty much everything was going well.

There were a few problems at first with people FLYING all over the place, but after a while, they got used to sticking to certain RULES in the air so everyone could be safe.

And flying shoes really are as fun as they look.

You'll never be late for school again. (Ever!)

You can see over TALL people's heads.

(No problem at all.)

You can reach for stuff that's up high. (Easy-peasy.)

AND if you ever get chased UP a tree by a dog again—DON'T PANIC.

Escaping couldn't be easier (and it beats climbing a tree).

Wendy was allowed a few comforts from home in Shoe Prison.

Meanwhile . . .

Wilberforce Wedge, on vacation, was enjoying the

news of his gruesome twin sister's downfall

(a little too much).

**SHOO DOING
THE SHOE SHUFFLE**

Over to you, Liz Pichon . . .

Make it snappy; it's been a long book.

OK, here goes . . . (I've got a lot of people to thank). Firstly, HUGE thanks to my publisher, Scholastic, who have worked so hard to put this book together. Catherine Bell, Miriam Farbey, and Dick Robinson. To my brilliant editors, thank you for your patience and expert EYES: Sam Smith, Lauren Fortune, Abigail McAden, Genevieve Herr, and Pete Matthews. To the fabulous art folk: Andrew Biscomb, Jason Cox, and my sister Lyn (who came to the rescue as ever!). Thanks to Hannah Love, Penelope Daukes, Toni Pelari, Claire Tagg, and all the team for getting the book OUT into the world. MASSIVE thanks to my wonderful agent (of over twenty years), Caroline Walsh, and also to Georgina Ruffhead for your expert guidance. BIG love to my family, who put up with me during my deadlines. Mark, Zak, Ella, and Lily—I love you loads xxxxxxx.

When Liz was little, she loved to draw, paint, and make things. Her mom used to say she was very good at making a mess (which is still true today!).

She kept drawing and went to art school, where she earned a degree in graphic design. She worked as a designer and art director in the music industry, and her freelance work has appeared on a wide variety of products.

Visit her at LizPichon.com.